THE PERSEUS PROTOCOL

A CAL SHEPARD THRILLER

JT SAWYER

Thank you for buying this book! I hope you enjoy reading it as much as I enjoyed researching and writing it.

Join my email list if you would like to receive notifications on future releases or a FREE copy of the Cal Shepard short story, *Lethal Conduct,* which recounts Cal's harrowing mission in North Africa with his former search & destroy unit.

PROLOGUE

DHAKA, **Bangladesh**

THE CAFÉ across the street from Cal had an air of defeat, its faded brick walls covered in flaking white paint that reluctantly clung to the sad façade. Lining the narrow sidewalks around the two-story building were countless peddlers, sitting resignedly on blankets adorned with wares ranging from knock-off jewelry to assorted fruits to spice-filled samosas. Nearly all of them were older teenage boys, markedly dispirited and whose skin glistened from a weeks-old patina of sweat and grime.

From his perch atop a shabby three-story apartment complex, Cal scanned the streets to the north and south again, his eyes settling for a moment on a young man in a tattered blue-and-red tie-dye shirt with a small monkey on his shoulder, entertaining some European tourists with three juvenile cobras nestled in ceramic pots whom he seemed to command to rise at will with his hand gestures, knowing that the cobras had most likely had their fangs forcibly removed. Cal had seen the reptilian performance plied by con-men in Africa and India before while several pickpockets at the rear worked the enthralled crowd of unsuspecting tourists. As if sensing his scrutiny, the young rhesus monkey on the street performer's shoulder squawked, momentarily glancing towards Cal as if to make sure he would remain silent about the coming ruse.

Everybody's gotta make a living with the skills they're given, it seems.

Cal's gaze drifted back to the crowded intersection near the café. He watched a tall bearded man scamper between the auto-rickshaws and bicycle-pulled carts on the street before sauntering into the establishment.

He was as Cal remembered him, with deep furrows on his face and a dark tan that made his skin resemble parched driftwood. A lifetime spent in jungle ops in the Southeast Asia division of the CIA changed men into something other than human at times, and Cal was sure the man had a predator's keen awareness, probably knowing he was already being surveilled.

Cal glanced around at the other rooftops then along the sidewalk, not picking out anything unusual. He retraced his steps back to the stairwell, trotting down to the ground level and pausing in the open doorway to make another scan of the bustling humanity rushing past him, then he lowered his frayed ballcap and meandered across the two-lane street, darting between bicycles, rolling food carts and other pedestrians moving like a unified school of fish.

Searing heat coupled with the incessant throng of humanity around him created an oppressive curtain of pungent humidity that felt like he was parting a wet blanket with each step.

Entering the café, Shepard moved with purpose towards

the stairwell at the back, carefully plodding up the splintered wooden planks that passed for steps to a small shaded dining area on the open rooftop.

He had scouted the location two days ago upon arriving in Dhaka during a downpour, which was hard to imagine now given the searing heat.

Shepard strode by a young Thai couple sitting at a round table finishing their breakfast, then past a well-dressed Anglo woman squawking on her iPhone about the new laws regarding international trade.

Cal casually sat down at the last table across from the bearded man, who removed his sunglasses, his crow-footed eyes staring at the younger man across from him.

"You look like hell, Cal." He pushed one of the cups of chai tea in the center of the table towards Shepard, who waved it off.

"Thanks. Great to see you too after all these years."

"Our mutual acquaintance wasn't sure if you'd show up or not, figuring you'd reconsider his offer, whatever that was, and go it alone."

"And how did he look?"

The man leaned back, glancing up at a cluster of cumulus clouds beyond the edge of the shade canopy. "More worried than I can ever recall."

"That's just his normal waking state." Cal glanced at the faint outline of something imprinted against the man's blue button-up shirt, which hung loosely over his waist. "You still packin' that old .45?"

"At the very least. Knowing the trouble you usually attract, I wondered if a small arsenal was necessary." He took a sip of his chai tea then tapped his finger on the side of the cup. "Cal, I heard about what happened to your wife back in the States. I'm sorry for your loss, old friend."

Cal nodded, averting his eyes momentarily. "Thank you."

He had used the man before as a liaison for trusted intel drops in other hot spots in Malaysia and Indonesia, and he was one of the few trusted assets left that he could turn to for help with what he was about to undertake in India. Plus, Cal's former mentor Neil Patterson on the other side of the globe had assured him that the man would deliver the goods as promised. On that note alone, he felt some sense of comfort.

The man put his right hand on a folded newspaper on the table, sliding it across to him. "Everything you need— secure funds, a safehouse location, weapons caches and further assets in the region. *He* indicated that the password is from a particular bird of prey you both witnessed in action in the Tunisian desert two years ago coupled with your old call-sign from that mission."

Cal nodded, pushing aside his untouched cup of tea and pulling the newspaper closer, removing the silver flash-drive in the center. He ran his fingers along the edges as if it were a religious amulet then put it in his pocket.

"And you were already compensated, I trust?" he said to the man.

"Everything is taken care of, my friend." He finished his tea then stood up, extending his leathery hand. "I wish you well and hope we meet again under less trying circumstances."

"Likewise, but it seems like those are the only kind of circumstances in our line of work." Cal shook his hand then watched the lithe figure trot down the steps. From his perch above the café, Cal saw the man melt into the pedestrian traffic on the busy street, leaving him alone once again. It was a feeling that Cal never used to despise, but now he was cut off from his country, the agency and the life he once knew back home.

Home...what the hell does that even mean anymore?

He got up, walking to the edge of the roof, staring out at the horizon, wishing he could relinquish the past and what it was now demanding of him.

1

NORTHERN INDIA

FOUR WEEKS Later

THE INCESSANT SQUEAKING of the bent ceiling fan in the communications room ahead was the only thing that cloaked the sound of grit under Shepard's boots as he moved along the narrow hallway towards the technician standing with his back to the entrance.

Just as the man turned to leave, Shepard rushed forward, closing the distance and entwining his arms around the technician's scrawny neck. The constricting motion from a rear-naked choke quickly cut off the blood supply to the man's carotids, causing him to grow limp.

Cal lowered the figure to the ground, resting his head on the cement floor. He moved to the control panel on the desk, typing on the computer console until he located the land-line phone numbers for the past seven days for the Punjab district. After scanning a long list of analog phone numbers, his eyes fixated on a particular numeric string. He clicked on it, pulling up the dates, times and location for the caller.

Shepard removed his burner phone, taking several photos, then closed out the program. He leaned back to check on the technician, whose groans were indicating the man would awaken soon.

Cal hopped from his seat, removing some zip-ties from his pack, then secured the man's hands to the rusty water pipe beside a drinking fountain.

He returned to the computer, lowering his tattered daypack onto the desk, glancing at the array of old hard-drives and outdated software plugged into the mainframe.

His eyes darted to the pack then over to the computer again. Shepard looked down at his watch, knowing he had a finite amount of time to retreat before the Indian military was notified of a breach at one of their outlying facilities in the countryside.

He licked his lips, hastily plucking a small insulated case from his pack, the insides lined like a mini Faraday cage. He removed the hard-drive containing the Perseus source code. For a second, he let his hand linger on the black box as the memory of its discovery at Stephen Burke's Virginia estate weeks ago floated across the jagged landscape of his weary brain.

Originally designed to detect social and political anomalies related to potential assassination attempts, political coups and terrorist strikes, the Perseus software had been a multi-million dollar undertaking sanctioned at the highest levels of the U.S. intelligence community, but to Shepard, the black box felt like it had become an immovable chest, tethering him to the anguish of his life back in the States. He pushed away the thoughts of that former life, like he was looking through an opaque lens at a distant world. He submerged the faces of those he loved, forcing his senses back to the present.

With the source code in his possession, he needed to find the one person that Stephen Burke had indicated could help Shepard recalibrate the device. Without the source code, the Perseus program would never come to complete fruition.

After weeks of fruitlessly following breadcrumbs around the Indian coastline, he'd had little luck in tracking down the mysterious Terry Zemenova who had caused him to be in this country in the first place. She was the cyber-colleague of Burke's who was somehow connected with the development of Perseus and was instrumental in completing the remaining steps that Burke revealed were necessary to fully activate Perseus. Now, the data from this comms facility would hopefully enable him to zero in on her location. He had weighed his next action considerably, wondering what events he would be setting in motion.

I made a promise to you, Stephen, to finish what you started, but you may not like how I accomplish that.

Cal inserted the thick cord from the black box into the main computer, glancing at the monitor as rows of alphanumeric code began floating across the screen. He had discovered upon arriving in India weeks ago that his first, and only, attempt at accessing the black box had caused the device to hijack open communications sources, in his case his encrypted burner phone. Now, he was hoping to use that technological liability as an asset to identify and draw out other players whom Neil Patterson indicated would be on the hunt for the missing source code. If Shepard could pinpoint them and control the stage of conflict, he would have a chance of fulfilling Burke's last wish and getting out of this country alive.

But after sixteen years in black-ops, he was painfully aware that controlling a conflict of any kind, especially on foreign soil, was wishful thinking and something best left on the planning table. The reality was that combat and chaos were two inextricably connected forces that often spun out of control once the bullets started flying downrange.

His eyes followed the flow of alphanumeric code on the monitor for a few minutes, each line showing, what was to him, the same gibberish. The overhead lights flickered, and the ceiling fan stopped circulating momentarily.

A second later, a red icon appeared on the monitor, indicating that the black box was aborting the attempt, citing an incompatible system.

Cal yanked out the ether-cord, feeling the device, noticing it was only mildly warm. He returned it to the Faraday case then zipped up the pack, flinging it on his shoulder then getting up and stepping over the legs of the groaning technician before retracing his steps down the corridor.

Pausing beside the unconscious guard slumped on the ground, he slowly pried open the door and scanned the muddy parking area ahead.

Cal stepped out and trotted around the back side of the building, crouch-sliding down the grassy slope until he arrived at a deer trail, then jogging for a quarter-mile towards his jeep hidden in the dense underbrush.

Climbing inside, he stowed the backpack in a steel lockbox bolted to the floor then attached the padlock.

He would need time to triangulate the location of the phone number he'd retrieved and knew that it would have to wait until he was well on his way on the last train out of Barnala, twenty miles to the south.

Cal started the engine and engaged the clutch, backing up over the trampled foliage then veering to the right and heading down the old logging road, the first of many convoluted steps that all had to unfold if his mission was to succeed and he was to have any chance of regaining some semblance of a life, though he was certain he had no idea what that would look like.

2

AN HOUR LATER, storm clouds were gathering along the northern horizon, and Cal picked up speed, hoping to get off the already slick roads before they turned into a goopy mess.

The parked convoy of three trucks in the valley below barely caught his attention as he raced along the hillside road that was the singular path up to the comms facility he'd just breached. It was just a fortuitous opening in the jungle foliage beside a cliff that afforded a glimpse into the horrors unfolding below.

He came to a slow stop then backed up until he had a clear view of the valley. The large cargo trucks were all stopped at odd angles like they had barely avoided crashing into one another. All of them were adorned with the white-and-red logo of a foreign aid group whose workers operated in this remote section of Northwest India.

To the rear of the last truck were two women and eight children huddled beside the bullet-riddled bodies of a half-dozen males.

Three armed men wearing tattered shirts and shorts

stood behind the survivors while two more men crawled out from the cargo bay of the first truck, carrying armloads of medical supplies and HAM radio components.

Shepard glanced down at his watch again, knowing the last train out of this region was departing in ninety minutes and he needed to be on it.

I'll call this in when I get back to town. The local authorities will have to handle it.

He engaged the clutch and shifted into first gear then resumed his route down the hillside. Cal had heard about the bandits from the Naja clan operating in these sparsely populated areas. Most of them simply held up convoys and pilfered the goods, leaving the passengers unharmed, but stories also abounded about the scourge of human trafficking to the north that had swelled in recent years.

The local cops or Indian Army will handle this. Just keep driving. You can't get involved.

He had his own personal security issues to contend with, since the area would be swarming with military personnel sent to investigate the break-in at the comms facility. Soon roadblocks would be in place, making escape even more challenging than it was already going to be.

Descending the last switchback, he came to a halt at a Y in the narrow road. The left route led to the train depot in Barnala. To the right was the valley and the ill-fated convoy survivors.

The logical part of his brain instructed him to take the path to the left, while his gut instincts were already forcefully yanking him to veer right.

"Don't do this, Cal. Just radio it in from the train station."

His stomach coiled up as he clutched the stick-shift, feeling like the air around him was about to erupt in a downpour.

3

TWENTY-THREE-YEAR-OLD CLARA FLETCHER encircled her arms around the remaining survivors of her convoy, the smallest children clutching her legs as the band of murderous thieves rifled through the crates and personal belongings in the back of the last truck.

She felt like vomiting, her heart racing and her hands still shaking from the mass execution of her male colleagues strewn about the ground. As the medical coordinator for this district, she had encountered her share of bandits and petty thieves during the past three years of service, but nothing on this scale.

Not outright murder and savagery.

An hour ago, she was humming songs with the children in her care. Now, she was reeling in shock from the brutal attack and the loss of her friends. The feeling of sadness intensified as she looked around at the other captives beside her, knowing the merciless thieves were most likely connected with a group of slave-traders rumored to be operating in the foothills.

Growing up in a rough Boston neighborhood had

provided her with the mental toughness to endure the rigors of being an aid worker in a remote village, but nothing had prepared her for the raw brutality that she had just witnessed.

A part of her wanted to rush forward, lunging at the armed goon sitting near the tailgate and pummeling him with her fists, but she tempered her rage, knowing that now wasn't the time to unleash her rage.

She had enough command of the language to understand the men's comments about where they were going next, and the crudely tattooed image of a black cobra on their forearms indicated they were members of the Naja clan, a group of organized mobsters that controlled this region of India. She felt her throat become parched, knowing they were probably going to be taken to the lawless regions along the Pakistan border to the west and sold to one of the human traffickers.

A skinny man in a soiled tank top and shorts strode towards them, the black wispy tuft of hair on his chin resembling floss.

He stood before the group, scrutinizing the women and young girls like he was inspecting livestock. He grabbed the wrist of a ten-year-old girl clinging to Clara's pant leg, prying her away as she wailed. The woman rushed forward, pulling the girl free and shoving her behind her.

The man tilted his head, giving her an odd glance. He looked at the two men to his right while grinning and muttering something that made them all laugh.

He lurched forward, grabbing Clara's blond hair and pulling her towards him. As terrified as she was, Clara didn't resist, instead using the momentum to send her knee into his groin. The man let go, groaning as he collapsed to the ground. The large goon to the right rushed in, sending a vicious backhand across Clara's cheek. He balled his fist, coiling it back for a strike when a loud voice resounded behind them.

A tall man with a red button-up shirt and a gold watch on his bony wrist yelled at the others to disperse and get the trucks ready. He slapped the young man with the bearded chin, waving him off, then motioned to Clara to get her group loaded into the last truck.

"We are part of an aid network throughout India and Southeast Asia and are protected under international law. Wherever you are taking us, our absence will be reported and the military will come for us."

He grinned, pointing to three black devices with exposed wires lying alongside the road. "No GPS...no find you."

ADESH PATEL HAD PROCURED FAR MORE merchandise in this raid on the aid group than in any past venture he could recall during the past four years since rising to the head of the band commanding this region of jungle.

He and his small crew alternated between hasty strikes upon unsuspecting aid and farm convoys and pickpocketing efforts in the tourist towns to the south. But it was the goods they obtained from these larger truck convoys that would keep them basking in opium and women for the next month. Most importantly, this would bolster his tarnished image in the eyes of his father, who controlled the black market as the head of the Naja network that ruled the northern half of India.

Adesh glanced down at the tan legs of the captive girl sitting between him and the driver as they bobbed along the muddy road. To him, the teenager was nothing more than a commodity, and he had already calculated that her innocent face and delicate figure would be worth two new AKs with the slavers along the Pakistan border. That alone helped to partially restrain the desire burning in him to extend his caress further.

He ran his fingers along the side of her cheek, wiping away a tear. Adesh slid his hips closer to hers but nearly slammed into the front dashboard as the driver brought the truck to a sudden stop.

Both men stared at the jeep blocking the road thirty feet ahead. It was angled slightly with its hood ajar, an open toolbox and a jack resting on the ground beside the front tire.

Adesh ordered the driver out to inspect the other vehicle as he removed the weathered Makarov pistol from his belt.

4

IF THERE HADN'T BEEN two personnel on duty at the comms facility, Shepard would already be back at the train station and would never have happened across the unfortunate aid workers.

Being without the resources of an intel team and his old unit had crippled his abilities, forcing him to resort to old-school tactics of information gathering and surveillance that were causing him to stick his neck out in a foreign country and abandon his normal precautions.

Though right now, the outcome of these convoy survivors outweighed any logic. He had worked with and assisted many international aid groups in the Middle East and Africa over the years and found many of the younger recruits to be driven by a passion that sometimes left little room for common sense.

By the looks of the logo on the trucks, he was sure this was a subsidiary of a U.S.-based rescue group called Humanitarian Emergency Response that had helped establish refugee camps near the Syrian border when he and his search-and-destroy team were tracking down a terrorist cell two years ago. One of the aid workers was an embedded CIA asset who had helped them with their exfil out of the country, but Shepard doubted he would have any such luck with the two older women he had seen in this group.

Still, if they've been living out here under such rugged conditions, they have to be some damn hardy souls. Or just foolish.

From the edge of the treeline thirty yards from his jeep, he saw the stout driver waddle out from the truck and slowly approach the jeep. Cal squeezed off a single round from his suppressed HK pistol, splintering apart the seated man's skull beside the girl. He quickly swept his weapon to the left, shooting two rounds into the burly man near the jeep, dropping him against the tailgate.

He heard the girl shriek then waved at her to stay inside, raising his index finger to his lips.

As the drivers in the two other trucks began emerging with their AKs, Shepard sprung up, rushing out from the forest while shooting a rapid burst of rounds at the men, dropping them with multiple headshots.

A blur of movement from the tailgate of the second truck refocused his attention. A bare-chested figure with an SKS dropped down behind the rear tire, leveling his rifle. Shepard fired two rounds into the man's leg above the left kneecap, causing the lanky figure to collapse on his side.

The man's momentary wailing ended abruptly with a final round that punched through his forehead. A sudden rush of movement filled Shepard's vision as another figure lunged from the darkness of the truck bed, sending him to the ground. The lanky thug clenched Shepard's waist, shoving his pistol hand down, causing him to drop the weapon. The man's maniacal eyes widened as he clutched both of his hands around Shepard's throat.

Cal drove a spear hand into the side of the man's

trachea, causing him to release his grip and recoil. Cal used the momentum to roll to the side, removing the fixed blade on his belt and slamming it into the man's neck repeatedly, then arced the weapon up in a reverse slice across the neck, severing the right carotid.

Shepard scurried to the left, retrieving his pistol as two more men rushed out with their AKs from the last vehicle.

5

CLARA SAT in the back of the covered truck, the coarse rope restraints abrading her wrists, which slightly blotted out the throbbing of her bruised cheekbone.

Ten minutes after leaving the valley where they had been ambushed, the truck had come to a sudden stop. Even the surly thug guarding them seemed surprised, so when he hastily exited, she motioned for the others to huddle closer to her, whispering to all of them to undo one another's binds.

"Fleeing into the jungle right now is our best option for escaping, but we need to split up. Each of you go in pairs with one older and one younger child. Then run and keep running. I will..."

She paused, all of their eyes glancing to right at the canvas walls suspended over the rafters of the truck bed as a series of muffled pops broke through the air.

Clara felt her heart punching through her ribs as she heard a high-pitched shriek that reminded her of the owls that tore into the fleeing rabbits at night around their jungle basecamp.

The younger children pressed in closer to her. She narrowed her eyes, shuffling in a crouch-walk to the tailgate, then slowly leaned out, peering beyond the side. The guard was lying on his back, his glassy eyes staring up as blood leaked from a hole in the side of his head.

Her pulse quickened as she hopped down, grabbing the weathered SKS rifle off the ground then motioning for the others to quickly exit.

A gravelly voice to the rear startled her. "You're better off getting out of here in these trucks than heading into the jungle. There'll be other bandits out here soon, is my guess."

She swung around, clutching the rifle, which she leveled at the bearded man's chest. Clara glanced down at the pistol that he had lowered to his side.

"You should slide back the safety on that rifle when it comes time to use it."

She glanced down at the barrel, tracing her eyes up to the safety near the bolt and sliding it aside.

"You're American. Who are you?" she said.

The man didn't seem to register the question, walking past her then leaning over the body of the dead man and plucking the cellphone from his jeans and the walkie-talkie off his belt.

He scanned the jungle on either side, still unresponsive to her query but acknowledging the sorrow in her eyes. "I'm sorry for the loss of your colleagues back there, but we should get moving in case there's more of the goon squad on the way."

"What are you doing out here? There aren't too many outsiders this far north."

He thrust his chin up towards the serpentine road on the hillside. "I was just driving back to town and saw your group being rounded up by these guys."

"There's nothing up that way except an old electrical facility or something. That's a dead-end road."

This looks like the dead-end road to me.

"There's a shortcut of sorts that I was taking."

"And you always travel with a gun with a silencer when you're out on a drive in the sticks?" She glanced at his weapon. "My dad was a cop in Boston, and the only people I heard of having weapons like that were drug dealers and hitmen."

He glanced at his watch for the tenth time. His posture clearly said that he didn't have time to stay and chat. He moved up to the driver's door of the third truck, opening it and yanking out the lifeless figure inside.

"Take this vehicle. It's got the least damage to the inside."

She moved closer, still clutching the SKS as the other girls poured out of the rear of the truck, sending shocked looks at the bodies splayed around the vehicles then peering up at the stranger.

"What about you?" she said.

"You can follow me out for a while, then I'll split off at the fork by the river a few miles to the south. Just keep taking the road you're on for ten miles and you'll run across a small town."

"I know the area, thanks."

Clara lowered the rifle, removing the sweat-soaked bandanna she used to hold her hair up and wiping away the bone splinters and blood on the front seat of the truck. She waved at the oldest girls to get back into the rear while the four smallest climbed inside the cab.

"I only have one request...don't relay anything about what happened here just yet. Wait until you are back at your encampment to explain what went on. The other bandits connected with these guys could be listening in. That's probably how they knew you'd even be out here in this exact location."

He handed her the radio. "Tell your boss or whoever runs the show that he should use code words for your convoys and locations rather than actual names or geographic indicators. Look up what the Brits have done with their aid groups in Africa and you'll find a wealth of security protocols that will hopefully prevent something like this from happening again."

As the man headed towards his jeep, she said, "Have a name?"

"Jake."

She frowned in disbelief.

"Thanks, whoever you are," said Clara. "This could have ended much differently for us if you hadn't shown up."

He held up the dead man's cellphone, which had just illuminated with a fresh text. "It's not over yet, so get a move on it. These guys probably have a pretty good network of sentries in these parts, so I would steer clear of this region for a few months and tell the top dog in charge at Humanitarian Response to reconfigure your travel routes ASAP."

"How'd you know we were with HR? That's our parent organization behind the scenes back in the States. You with the government?"

He seemed to weigh the question as he closed the hood of his jeep then shouted back to her, "Nope."

JUST OVER AN HOUR LATER, he boarded the train, heading to the rear seat on the last car and slumping down. He was worn out and famished, but his desire to scroll through the phone records he'd photographed at the comms facility overrode his physical needs.

In between glances at the images on his phone, he glanced out the window at the last rays of sunlight pouring over the jungle hillsides.

He shook his head.

What am I even doing here?

In another reality, he would be eagerly awaiting the arrival of his baby girl into the world with his wife Cassie. Instead, he was a fugitive, cut off from the country and agency he had dutifully served for over fifteen years.

He just wanted to find a quiet, untrammeled part of the globe and disappear. After four weeks of fruitless searching for Theresa Zemenova, he was wondering if there was any point in locating the woman.

Cal resumed scanning the images of the landline phone records, hoping his latest efforts would pay off and he'd be able to pinpoint her location.

This has to work. He balled a fist. *This has to end soon.*

He glanced at the backpack next to him.

Is this all there is now?

To live on the run.

Alone.

Waiting for someone like me to center the crosshairs on the back of my fucking head.

He wasn't sure what terrified him more, the latter thought or that a part of him was beginning to welcome it.

AT SUNRISE THE NEXT MORNING, two jeeps came to a halt thirty yards from the two derelict trucks on the winding road. Eight armed men stepped out with their rifles, scanning the dead bodies on the ground then sweeping their gazes along the thick treeline.

Rohan Patel, the oldest figure in the group, pushed past his men, his eyes fixated on the cab of the first truck. He moved up beside it, staring in through the open door at the dead man slumped on the dashboard.

The other henchmen moved up near their boss, growing silent and giving each other nervous glances as they stared at Patel's dead son inside.

Patel made a fist, slamming it against the driver's seat. He scowled, glancing back over his shoulder. "Check the other men. See if there are any clues on who did this."

He felt like he had been disemboweled, waves of rage racing over him. Not since the war with his three other rivals twelve years ago when he declared victory over this region of India had anyone dared to strike at his family or his supply line. The fifty-two-year-old leader of the Naja clan held an iron grip on the black market and opium trade over the two-hundred-mile territory from the Pakistan border to New Delhi, and he intended to keep it that way.

Patel wasn't as concerned that his brash and drug-addicted son Adesh had been killed as he was about the image of weakness it would send to the other crime bosses in India.

If someone thinks they can hit a small convoy of my guys deep in the heart of my own territory, then what's stopping them from making a move on my holdings in Delhi?

He stepped down, glancing at the logo for the international aid group on the truck door then looking back up into the glassy eyes of his dead son.

You idiot. I told you never to hit the relief groups. Now, I will have to bribe someone high up in INTERPOL to keep this quiet.

His oldest son, Sai, walked up beside him, holding a

bootlegged version of a Go-Pro camera in his hand. "Father, you need to see this. Found this on the dash of the second truck. Looks like the previous driver from the aid group was recording during their trip."

Patel stepped closer, watching the footage from the halfway point after the assault on the convoy by a bearded white man.

Patel raised an eyebrow, watching the figure deftly eliminating the gangster's crew.

Whoever he is, he's a professional. Is one of the other gang leaders trying to make a move on me, or was this guy sent by my competitors in Pakistan?

He grabbed the camera, rewinding it and zooming in on the man's face. He held up the image to the others who had huddled around him.

"I want this son-of-a-whore located...alive. Scour the countryside and surrounding villages." He grabbed Sai's arm. "Get that image uploaded and circulated throughout the rest of our network. I want you to see to it personally that this guy is found."

Patel glanced at the second truck and the bodies on the ground. "Put the dead in the jungle, then I want two of you to take a truck to the relief group across the valley. Someone from that camp will know what happened here, but be discreet with your inquiry."

"What about Adesh?" said a tall man in a red tank-top.

Patel waved his meaty hand at the dense treeline. "Drag him into the jungle with the others. The leopards will take care of him." He shot a glance into the cab of the truck. "Then again, with all the drugs in his system, he'll probably still be intact a year from now."

6

SENATOR NICHOLAS EDGEWORTH couldn't remember an October this chilly, and he tugged on his leather gloves as he sat on the park bench, the frigid wind managing to slice through his black overcoat.

At the sound of someone on his right approaching, he didn't bother to look at him, figuring his nearby security detail would have already intercepted the individual if it wasn't who it was supposed to be.

"You couldn't have picked a museum or library to meet in?" he said with his characteristic Southern accent.

"The cold keeps a person sharp, and right now, I need you focused," said Director of National Intelligence Jason Begley as he sat down.

"I have a feeling I can already tell what you wanted to talk about."

"Good, then I can spare all the excruciating detail."

Begley rested his bare hands on his knees. "The Magellan program is nearly ready to go live."

"A month behind schedule. Are you sure this time?" The senator kept his gaze on a flock of pigeons on the brown grass ahead.

"Without a doubt. Four more days, and it'll be up and running across the country. All I need you to do is to use your usual persuasion skills to convince the House Appropriations Committee to greenlight the next round of budget expenditures. That will enable the private satellite firm I've been working with to move beyond Magellan's initial testing phase."

"Just remember, the committee was sold on Magellan because they think it's a terrorist surveillance system for use by the agency abroad, not on our own soil for domestic insurrectionists. If they or the media get wind of a computer that is targeting our own citizens, based on parameters *you* designed, then standing before the DOJ will be the least of our problems." The stout man swiveled towards Begley. "I'm putting a lot of stock in you pulling this together before you leave office in a week."

"*This* is what's enabling me to leave office, Senator, and what will fill your personal coffers. With the forthcoming attack I have planned, the Senate will have no issues signing off on the domestic surveillance program with the software we stripped out of the old Perseus program."

"I thought you said that program disappeared after Burke's death?"

"It did, at least what was in his possession at the time, but it was in our contract that he provide me with a monthly update on his software developments with Perseus, so I had an older version that we've been salvaging for Magellan."

"And how is this not going to be traced back to the previous funds that the government spent on Perseus?"

"With Magellan in the hands of my private company, it won't draw suspicion as it would if it were being wielded by one of our intelligence agencies. It's totally compartmentalized within another operation of mine, complete with its own off-the-books staff and satellite contracting firm, away from prying eyes in D.C."

Begley leaned back, resting his arm on the back of the bench. "There won't be any trace back to you or our other intel agencies while you still reap the personal rewards." He patted the older man on the shoulder. "Don't worry, Nick, you and Mrs. Edgeworth will still be able to retire early down in Bermuda."

"And you don't have any clue what happened with the original Perseus program that Burke created? It's a little unsettling to think that Magellan may have a rival hidden in the shadows somewhere that could undermine all of this. If that cyber-device was designed to detect political anomalies and assassination attempts, then it could expose you, me and Magellan with the tactical strike you're planning."

"Senator, just remember that you are just a rook, watching from the end of the chessboard. Of course, I'm aware of what's at stake, and I'll have the source code and anyone connected to it buried shortly." He ran his hand through his hair as the senator gave him an irritated glance.

"Nothing turned up on the investigation of the theft at Burke's corporate headquarters on the evening he and his staff were vaporized at his country estate," said Begley. "That tells me that someone very skilled in espionage was involved with the removal of the mainframes. There's just no way to get that sheer amount of hardware out the back door, literally, without setting off a sophisticated and layered security system. But I will locate them eventually and put them in a hole at a black site so deep that even God won't be able to find them."

The senator looked over at Begley, who was fifteen years his junior, wondering if he would have had the cunning and deceptiveness to pull off what the director of all the clandestine services was planning.

Edgeworth nodded, adjusting his wool hat as he watched a young woman in blue tights jogging in the distance with her dog.

Until Begley had approached him with the Magellan program last year, Edgeworth figured he still had another ten years of slogging in the halls of D.C. Now, with things finally underway with their lucrative deal, he would be able to finish out his term by next spring and never have to cope with an East Coast winter again.

"I'm assuming you already have some home-grown terror groups in mind to begin targeting once Magellan is operational?"

Begley tapped his left fingers on the bench. "Trust me, there's no shortage of those. There's a radical militia organization called Sentinel, which, ironically, is all about exposing government abuse of power. I've had one of my infiltration agents embedded in that group for some time, so they will be in play for the coming consumer electronics show, just as Magellan is completed."

"You sure you want to cut it that close? Why not wait until next month, once Magellan has been up and running a while, to work out any issues. That tech shit never goes smoothly in my experience."

"Because my replacement will be in office, and I need to have this underway by then. Besides, eliminating ninety percent of the software firms and their leaders at the conference will provide my new company with a considerable stake in the cyber industry."

Edgeworth re-adjusted his hat, pulling it down over the edges of his reddening ears. "Just make sure this leaves no question about the efficacy of having a domestic surveillance program. This assault needs to be a tear-jerker on the news with plenty of casualties. I don't want to sit on another commission trying to convince my colleagues why the Patriot Act is obsolete."

Begley shook his head. "Frankly, if our last two administrations had had any balls, we wouldn't even be in this predicament. President Weller has turned a blind eye long enough, thinking the only battles are the ones abroad so he doesn't piss off his constituents over here. Meanwhile, we keep seeing a tenfold increase in the amount of anti-government groups on our own shores."

Edgeworth pursed his lips. "Our current leadership is still stuck in a post-9/11 mindset that believes the war on terror is in the Middle East and Africa. That kind of thinking is going to lead to another Oklahoma City unfolding here, but the President is more concerned with his legacy right now. This is the very reason I agreed to sign off on your proposal in the first place, Jason...that *and* the Bermuda angle, of course."

"Well, it's hard to argue with the data that my intel agencies have compiled regarding the chatter within these extremist groups. Pouring a little fuel on their cause at their expense won't cause me to lose any sleep, and Magellan, in the hands of my private firm, will circumvent the restrictions faced by our government agencies. This was my original intent all along and why I signed off on Stephen Burke developing Perseus. He navigated through the software issues to iron out a superior technology for surveillance that our government would have taken another decade to complete with all its bureaucratic in-fighting."

Edgeworth leaned back. "And what criteria will be used for determining what constitutes an extremist?"

"You want this to be neat and tidy, Senator? It's not. Narratives that lead to violence rarely are, but the algorithms I've personally programmed into Magellan will make that determination. And since so many of these militant groups have migrated off standard social media platforms onto their own encrypted apps, my software will be able to penetrate those apps without the legalities currently hamstringing Homeland Security."

The senator stood up, readjusting the green scarf around his neck. "Just make sure you use Magellan to cleanse the forest floor of *all* the debris before a catastrophic wildfire takes place, torching the entire country. There's no point in having a patchwork approach when it comes to dealing with the lunatic fringe."

Begley leaned forward, nodding. "I knew there was something I liked about you from the get-go besides that Southern drawl, Senator."

BEGLEY WATCHED the stocky politician waddle away as his security detail slowly flowed in behind him. The cellphone in his pocket vibrated, and he pulled it out, seeing a number that filled him with mild trepidation.

"Something wrong? You weren't supposed to contact me until the weekend."

"It's not about Magellan. It's regarding a phone number we located while sifting through Stephen Burke's old records. It's from someone he spoke with consistently, beginning with the inception of Perseus nearly two years ago until a few weeks before his death this past summer."

"From where and by whom?"

"I don't have a user yet, but we dug deep on this, and the location is southern India, with most of the calls coming from the Mumbai region."

"That's the tech capital of India and where their intelligence services are located." He rubbed the back of his neck. "Could be someone in their government was working with Burke, or it could just be a colleague of his—a guy of his stature probably had regular conversations with other tech gurus in the cyber world."

"It's possible, but there's something else I just came across that makes me think otherwise. Something that you better examine in person."

"I have meetings lined up this afternoon, so just spit it out."

"You had better see for yourself. This isn't something I can send in a text due to the piss-poor quality of the image."

He stood up, muffling out an exhale, then walked briskly across the lawn to his car. "I'm on my way."

7

Virginia

A HALF-HOUR LATER, Begley pulled his black Audi in behind a tall building on the cusp of west Arlington. He trotted up the back steps that led to a steel door, removing a brass key and opening the external covering then typing in a six-digit security passcode. The thick steel door hissed open on its hydraulic struts. Begley stepped inside the ten-by-twenty room, which had a lone elevator door at the end.

He walked up, scrunching down slightly before the retinal scan on the right, and the doors slid open. Begley pressed the lone button on the panel, ascending the twenty-one floors in a building listed under one of his shell corporations.

Stepping out, he was greeted by his chief of cyber security, Dennis Palermo, whose pasty white face was paler than usual, which meant he should be concerned.

Begley made a beeline for Palermo's work station in the corner, barely acknowledging his other personnel at their desks or amongst the rows of mainframes occupying the left end of the spacious state-of-the-art facility.

The thirteen Magellan staff had all been culled by him during the past three months to put together his hastily assembled cyber unit. He had selected personnel based not only on their track record as analysts in the intelligence community but upon the additional leverage he discovered during his research phase into their personal and professional lives, whether related to deviant behaviors, work infractions, sexual misconduct, addiction or even their children's disabilities. For Begley, people under him were nothing more than a team of horses that had to be controlled under one whip, and this was the best lineup he could muster given his time constraints.

The one unbreakable rule in their unspoken contracts was that secrecy and anonymity were valued above all else. If any of them divulged their involvement with him or Magellan, their families would be eliminated. Conversely, their families would be financially compensated if they took their own lives if capture was imminent.

Such coerced loyalty ensured he was a feared leader, but he also felt like he was standing in a den of high-functioning sociopaths who could one day sell him out to a foreign competitor for the right price. Another reason he had assigned Palermo to provide audio and digital surveillance of the staff to circumvent any threats taking root.

In his many years of working within the intelligence community, Begley had established a wealth of connections with private defense firms that he was planning to tap to augment his capabilities with Magellan, and he would later use them to design a higher-functioning team.

Though Begley had led Senator Edgeworth to believe that Magellan was intended only for use on American soil, he was already planning to broker the technology amongst a network of colleagues who had left other intelligence agencies around the world. While Magellan's birthplace would be in the U.S., its use would spread throughout the globe, with Begley determining who would benefit from such a mass surveillance program. And once Magellan had an operational track record, he would expand his services into cyber offense, biometric analysis and enhanced digital security.

Begley stopped at Palermo's desk, folding his arms and flaring his eyebrows at the man.

"Well, what's so important that I had to come down here?"

The pudgy man pulled up a grainy image. "I discovered this while searching for that mystery caller in India. It was taken yesterday in the northwest part of the country."

The figure on the screen was lean with a black beard, his complexion more tan than Begley could recall from past encounters. He felt his pulse quicken as a flood of recent memories washed over him.

"Shepard. What the hell is he doing in the game? I thought he would have gone dark for good by now."

"Interestingly, he fits the description of a guy that rescued an international aid group from an assault not far from where this image was recorded. I picked up some chatter from the NSA feeds you routed into Magellan. And this guy was a few miles away from an old Indian government comms relay station that had been breached that same day."

"Anything specific mentioned with regard to the breach?"

"Nothing stolen—a database of landline phone records was accessed, and then it looks like an attempt to upload some software occurred, but it crashed the caveman facilities there."

He stood up, folding his arms. "It can't be a coincidence that Shepard reared his head in the same region where you tracked those old encrypted phone calls to Burke. It's probably safe to assume that he was the one at the comms facility, but what was he after?"

"I already pulled up the schematics on that place, and it's a secondary routing station that funnels data on analog phone calls for several provinces in the region northwest of New Delhi. It's all ancient tech that's in that building, but if you had the right hardware, you'd be able to zero in on the origin point of a particular phone number." Palermo swiveled in his seat, staring up at Begley.

"But here's the thing that really got my attention: The software recognition program I created to track any anomalies related to Perseus got pinged at the same time Shepard was in that comms facility."

Begley narrowed his eyes, leaning closer. "Shit, so he's been in possession of the source code all this time."

"He's not going to have the resources or personnel to pull off utilizing the source code in any capacity, so why risk exposing himself? Only the original Perseus mainframes would allow for that level of sophisticated tech to be unlocked."

"He's there for a reason, and if this caller from Burke's past is there too, they must be trying to figure out a way to utilize the device, or maybe they're lining up a buyer. Shepard's a cunning son of a bitch, so he could be planning to sell this to a rival intel agency for all we know." Begley paced around the work station.

He removed his cellphone, tapping an unmarked number. "Prep your team. I want you wheels-up within the hour. I have two targets that need acquiring. I'll have the location in India by the time you touch down."

Palermo swiveled around in his seat, staring up at Begley as the man tucked away his phone. "I'm not sure that's enough time for me to pinpoint both individuals."

"I only need one for starters, so begin with Shepard. I'll also notify our agency case officers, INTERPOL and border assets in India to cast a wide net. He won't get far."

"Don't you have a kill-or-capture order out on him?"

"The kill part is temporarily suspended as of now. I need to find out what he knows and get that device with the source code off the table. And I suspect that once we zero in on him, we'll also ensnare that caller."

He hoped things would unfold as smoothly as he had just portrayed, but he knew Shepard had been a ghost both during the manhunt for him following the aftermath of the explosion at Burke's estate and in the time that had elapsed since then. He needed the forthcoming attack at the conference in Philadelphia to unfold without a hitch. A horrific event on U.S. soil by domestic insurgents would be the catalyst that would thrust Magellan into the spotlight and cement his surveillance program as a necessary and welcome tool in the hands of his private firm.

Begley shuffled closer to Palermo's desk again. "And get an observation team on some of Shepard's former colleagues here in the U.S. and his former unit, wherever the hell they are. Look into recent activity on all their emails and phones. There are three people in particular that he may have had help from or been in touch with, so put a Level III surveillance package on them."

The cyber expert opened up a new screen. "Go ahead with their names."

"Neil Patterson, the former director of clandestine

services. He's retired now and living in Miami. I've already had him under surveillance for a few weeks after the disappearance of Perseus' mainframe, but expand the search radius on his daily world and see what turns up.

"Lynn Vogel is the other person. She works at Langley in Intel and was the targeter for Shepard's former unit." His eyes darted along the floor for a second. "She may actually be the key to finding him.

"Then there's Ryan Foley. He was the former field commander with the search-and-destroy unit Shepard headed up. Not sure what you'll turn up on him, as my guess is he's still working in black-ops outside of even my purview."

"How's that possible? I thought everyone in clandestine services answered to you," the man said as his plump fingers typed away.

"My predecessor once described the world of covert ops as compartments within Orwellian compartments, so you can be sure there are private contracting firms employing guys like Foley on our shores."

He was describing his own undertakings as much as what he suspected Foley was involved with since stepping down from commanding the Special Activities Division's search-and-destroy units two months ago.

An old hawk like Foley won't stay up on a perch for long. He'll need to be in the fight, one way or another...but working for who?

Begley also couldn't help recall that Foley's departure coincided with Shepard's disappearance.

If Shepard is in possession of the Perseus source code, he could be working under directives from Foley. But if Foley was the one who stole Perseus' mainframes from Burke's corporate offices, then why send Shepard to India...unless that mystery caller is indeed one of Burke's old colleagues versed in Perseus' technology?

The more he thought about the implications of Perseus being in Foley's hands, the more his stomach began coiling in knots. *If Perseus becomes fully operational, it will jeopardize everything I'm planning to do with Magellan and the coming attack. I have to kill that fucking program and anyone connected with it.*

Palermo typed in the data, his eyebrows flaring at the mention of the unit designation.

"So, that search-and-destroy shit was real. I thought that was just a story to make Shepard and his old team out to be phantom killers."

"It's very real and still active. But I also have my own units just like that, and they're about to make India a very dangerous place to be for a man on the run."

ONCE BEGLEY HAD LEFT the facility, Palermo slumped back in his chair, massaging his thumbs into his temples. He glanced longingly out the window at the distant clouds, trying to recall what the wind felt like upon his face.

During the past ninety days since beginning the Magellan project, he had spent most nights on the couch in the lounge area, and his waist size had ballooned from the frozen dinners and lack of physical activity.

When Begley had approached him last spring about heading up a new cyber division, he didn't realize it would also entail handling both cyber offense and defense, surveilling staff at their homes, and spending every waking hour optimizing the new Magellan software.

Any one of those roles was a full-time job, and he felt

like his mind was starting to fracture from the overload of numeric codes flashing across his eyes all day and the pressure of getting everything operational by the looming deadline for the pending attack in Philadelphia.

This shit had better pay off.

He took a bite from his half-thawed chicken burrito while analyzing the satellite images from India. When his eyes began blurring again, he pulled up a minimized screen, his tense cheeks immediately softening as he stared at a posh estate for sale overlooking the bustling streets of Rio de Janeiro.

8

Bulgaria

THE TRAIN HAD JUST LEFT the shipping yard as the woman and her two male companions increased their trot to a sprint, bolting from the shadows behind a warehouse towards the rear platform on the last car.

She leapt forward, clamping her hands on the rusty railing then pulling herself up and turning around to offer assistance to the men.

The moon was slipping out from the veil of thick clouds, and the outline of the small coastal city of Burgas along the Black Sea was now visible in the distance, becoming smaller with each kilometer of track as the train increased to full speed.

Samira removed the MP5 slung over her compact black pack, then slid down the night-vision goggles on her head as her companions did the same.

Once they were all equipped, she waited until the train entered the first concrete tunnel before placing the small shaped charge on the vault-like door to the train car. The three nocturnal boarders stepped to either side, facing away as she pressed the detonator, shattering the steel lock.

The trio flowed into the entrance, the woman in the lead, pointing her weapon at the armed guard to the right who was struggling to regain his footing after the blast.

Samira squeezed off two rounds into his face, his blood a green mist through her night vision, coating the crates behind him. She immediately swept the MP5 to the center of the aisle, shooting another guard in the inky black car who was training his AK in their direction.

"Get to work finding what we need. I'll cover the other door," she said in fluent Arabic to the two men behind her, who were already busy using bolt-cutters to open the nearest crates.

She pulled up the sleeve of her Neoprene jacket, scanning the GPS device mounted on her wrist. "Five minutes to the jump-off point, boys."

Sayyid, the bearded man behind her, flung down his bolt-cutters, removing a football-sized black box from the last case, holding it up in victory, causing a smile to form on the woman's tan face.

"Anything on these?" said Aden, the short man to her right.

"Yes," she said, tucking the device into her jacket. "They're military-grade hard-drives for storing weaponized malware, and these contain a particularly savage virus."

She thrust her chin at the dead guards. "Only the company was selling this shipment to the mob in Serbia, which is why these fellas were on board. Bulgaria has extremely *flexible* export regulations for military hardware, so it's become a gateway for international arms traffickers."

The bearded man waved his hand at the array of other

electronics equipment in the crates. "Too bad we don't have regular backpacks or we could liberate a few more devices."

"*Liberate*...I like that." She pushed him on the shoulder towards the rear door. "We need to go now."

They exited the car, standing on the platform, removing their night-vision gear and tossing it down. The woman leaned over the railing, seeing a black chasm approaching to the left of the train's engine in the distance.

Samira tapped on her ear-mic then slung her MP5 tightly across her chest. After an uncomfortable amount of static, a French-speaking voice crackled into her ear.

"Go ahead," said the man, an old Algerian.

"We are in position and will be on the ground in five minutes," she replied, switching mental gears from Arabic to French while removing a pair of impact-resistant goggles from her pocket and sliding them down over her eyes.

She kicked one leg over the railing, clutching the sides as her companions mirrored her moves, aligned side by side as the wind tugged at their tense bodies.

"I'm on the first bench of rock below where the canyon widens, as we discussed," said the pilot.

The jarring action of the train as it passed over the half-kilometer-long bridge caused her to tighten her already iron grip. She looked at the men to her left, whose faces were taut in the moonlight.

"Ten seconds," she yelled.

The maw of the massive canyon below seemed to create its own gravitational pull, and the floor three thousand feet below felt like it was disturbingly closer than she had visualized in their pre-mission planning. The rocky strata below was certainly different than the coastal region near Mumbai where they practiced their base-jumping training.

No turning back now.

As the train rounded the curve in the tracks in the center of the canyon, she sucked in a deep breath and closed her eyes, kicking off with her feet as she released her grip and descended in a dive.

The three-second countdown seemed like an eternity. She yanked her rip-cord, the parachute briefly sucking her back up. Samira forced out an exhale, seeing the comforting glimmer of two other chutes in the moonlight.

She tugged on the handholds controlling her descent speed, slowing her approach while angling her body slightly, then landed on a sandy shoulder of beach a hundred meters from the cliff face.

"You on the ground yet?" said the Algerian helicopter pilot.

The woman gathered her parachute, watching the train in the distance disappear into the Stygian night. Her companions moved up to her position, their faces paler than she could ever remember them being.

"Can we not do that again, sestra," said the bearded man.

"I'm with Sayyid," said the shorter man to her right. "He and I do not like heights and don't jump from planes on a regular basis like you, Samira."

She smiled. "Says the guy who was always climbing trees when we were kids."

"That's when Aden wasn't as fat as he is now," quipped Sayyid.

Aden made a fist, playfully waving it in front of his friend's face.

Samira pivoted her body slowly, scanning a route in the moonlight between the boulders. Her eyes darted ahead to a faint red flashing from the helicopter's strobe light.

"You on your way, or did you stop for lunch?" said the pilot into her earpiece.

"Inbound now. Be there in five minutes," she said.

"You're the boss, Viper," he said. "I'll be here as long as it takes."

"Why does he call you that name?" said Aden.

She glanced over her shoulder at the man. "It's a code name from another job...one I will have to change, I think."

"And the pilot worked with you?"

"Yes, he was an asset, but now he's just paying me back for a favor."

The three of them meandered through the jagged rock-piles, measuring their steps carefully to avoid wrenching an ankle.

To the two men, she was known by her real name, Samira, and all they knew was that she had, until recently, worked for a government agency in the U.S.

Her tactical know-how and fieldcraft skills were equaled only by her American friend Shepard, whom they had spent the past few weeks with in Mumbai, but the men were no strangers to war and chaos, having spent the past eight years as resistance fighters in their homeland of Syria.

Having grown up outside of Damascus with Samira, the men were taken in as boys by her family after their village was destroyed in the beginning of one of the first civil wars. Along with the surviving members of Samira's family, they had all spent three years together as refugees, bouncing around a multitude of relief camps, protecting each other while scavenging for life's bare necessities.

When Samira's father finally secured passage for them to Greece, their lives changed overnight. Two years later, when they were fifteen, they went to live with their aunt in England, but they would forever call Samira her family.

Now, here they were again, in another land far from home, enmeshed in a new struggle with their sestra and her American friend.

A few minutes later, the three of them arrived at the weathered Huey sitting silently on the lone flat spot along the rock steppes. As they climbed inside, the old Algerian fired up the engines.

He leaned back. "You get what you came for?"

She nodded, patting the protrusion in her vest pocket. "Yeah, we're good to go." Viper tried to relay confidence in her words, but she knew this was only one foothold in a long uphill trek that had to play out in the right order in the coming days or this whole trip would be for nothing.

As the helo ascended, she glanced at her two exhausted friends, praying they would remain out of harm's way but unsure herself of the variables beyond her control on the next leg of their mission.

She wondered where Cal was and if he had had any success in locating the elusive Theresa Zemenova. Viper recalled the soul-draining weariness etched on Cal's face and wondered how much longer he could keep pushing forward.

Hang in there, my friend. Things will line up soon.

His quest to find Zemenova and be free of the source code had since become her quest, but she knew she was also reaching her emotional limits to see this through and to further put Aden and Sayyid at risk.

Viper glanced at the rocky terrain below as it faded into forested hills, slumping back in the bench seat and closing her eyes.

9

Virginia

DERRICK NOLAN STOWED the Pelican case with the audio-eavesdropping equipment in it behind his seat then finished the last bit of black coffee in his cup.

He waited a few minutes for Jason Begley to enter the high-rise building on the outskirts of Arlington before exiting his SUV. From his vantage point on the street two blocks away, he saw the man park in the rear of the building then enter a key-coded door.

Odd that he hasn't had his usual two-man security detail with him here or at the park with the senator.

Nolan glanced up, counting the floors on the building and wondering why the director of national intelligence would be sneaking in through the back door of a medical technology firm.

The former Delta Force operator lowered the brim of his black baseball cap and left his sunglasses on as he entered the building, heading to the columnar directory in the middle of the lobby. After scanning the names, he glanced over at the security desk, where two guards were socializing with a young brunette woman who had just delivered them some cups of coffee.

To his left were the elevators and stairwell, which was choked with employees clad in skirts or suits. Most of them were fixated on their phones, which told him that this place didn't black out iPhone capabilities like some government buildings and R&D firms he'd been in before.

So, why is Begley here, and why go in through a rear entrance?

Nolan returned his gaze to the directory, examining the different departments, which were all connected in some form with medical or pharmaceutical devices.

He wanted to get in the elevator and scout a few of the floors, but dressed like he was in khaki pants, a black leather jacket and a baseball cap was only going to cause him to stand out.

When the brunette had left, Nolan walked to the security desk towards the burly man on the right, whose waistline was straining the limits on the lower recesses of his button-up shirt.

"Mornin', fellas. I was wondering if you could help me. I'm passing through town and wanted to look up an old buddy of mine who used to work for Regan Pharmaceuticals. His name is Mike Sheldon, but I'm not even sure if he's with the company anymore, and I don't have his cell number. Any way you could look him up and tell him I'm here?"

The man glanced at Nolan then plunked down in his swivel chair, pulling up the listing for Regan's offices on the fourth floor.

Nolan scanned the low-tech security monitors and primitive comms system behind the desk, seeing that each man was only armed with pepper spray and handcuffs.

The second guard stepped out from behind the desk, trotting to the lobby entrance to hold the double doors open for a delivery guy hauling in water jugs, both of them hashing out the details of last night's televised Steelers game.

Nothing seems out of the ordinary here, so what the hell is Begley up to? Hell, maybe he's just having an affair.

"Nobody by the name of Mike Sheldon, sorry. You could always head up there and ask Regan's receptionist what became of him," said the guard.

"Alright. Thanks, buddy. I appreciate it. Mike had talked about relocating to Jersey to be closer to his family, so he probably pulled up stakes."

He nodded at the man then headed towards the entrance, pausing in his tracks suddenly and swiveling his head at the directory again. Nolan felt his pulse quicken as he realized that the floor numbers on the roster only went as high as twenty in the twenty-one-story building.

He exited the building, heading down the street to his right then taking a circuitous route back to his vehicle.

Climbing inside, he removed his encrypted iPhone.

"Go ahead," said the gravelly voice of Colonel Ryan Foley.

"Begley and Senator Edgeworth were at a park discussing plans for a forthcoming strike of some kind involving a militant group called Sentinel. And your suspicions were right: Begley has some variant of Perseus in his possession, called it Magellan, only he's going to use it to target domestic terrorist groups that fit his profile."

"That sounds like the guy I know. He's been angling for

enhanced surveillance in our country for a long time. How close is he to completing this Magellan project?"

"I only heard mention of how he needs everything finalized by next week before he leaves office, something about an attack on a conference, but I couldn't pick up all the details."

"And Magellan...it's operational?"

Nolan glanced to his left at the high-rise building. "Not sure, but I'm pretty damn certain I know where it's headquartered. I used to hear about off-the-books DOD sites like this when my old team and I were testing out security on military bases around the world. My guess is that he's got Magellan hidden in plain sight to bypass scrutiny."

"And access?"

"Probably a designated elevator shaft with its own power source and, if I were him, I'd have a couple of Tier-One types on the other end, shooting anyone on sight who doesn't have clearance."

"I'll get our tech people on it. In the meantime, head back here and see what you can turn up on the blueprints on that place."

10

Twenty-Four Hours Later

Dugadda, India

Northeast of New Delhi

THE MERCENARY STOPPED the tan jeep in an alley on the outskirts of town where the last row of green plywood shacks seemed to melt into the lush jungle treeline.

He glanced down the litter-strewn pathway to the right then up at the stratus clouds hovering over the distant ridge of mountains.

"You sure this is the place?" he said with a slight accent into his earpiece.

"The target is there alright, probably right amongst the hundreds of other tourists. Been there since yesterday by the looks of the SAT images we were sent."

The mercenary peered up at the group of monkeys descending from the treetops onto the roofs, making their way towards some children who had just tossed out a bunch of food scraps.

He pulled the jeep forward, parking it along the crumbling edge of the curb, then stepped out. He donned a blue baseball cap then slung a small daypack over his shoulder. All he needed now was to let his mouth hang open and he'd fit right in with the other gawking American and European visitors milling around the streets two blocks away.

Despite its remoteness, this region of India had become a major draw in recent years due to the marketing efforts of the government and conservation groups to attract more eco-tourists bent on visiting the nearby tiger reserves and the last stands of virgin tropical forest in the northern mountains.

But the man had hardly noticed the jungle scenery and exotic wildlife on the three-hour drive through the green hell and stifling humidity, his mind lasered in on the objective at the road's terminus.

Two weeks earlier, he had received notice from his employer abroad that the target had been sighted in India. A hasty meeting with his five-man team at their rally site in Bangladesh to retrieve their weapons, then a short flight on a private charter into New Delhi had all been financed by his employer, who was extremely determined to see results at any cost.

But fruitless scouring along the coastal cities had yielded little. In a country with few public security cameras to hack, they had been forced to resort to old-school methods of pounding the pavement in their search.

That all changed four days ago when his employer had begun providing satellite imagery from sources unknown.

That was when the hunt began. The subject had briefly been spotted boarding a train originating in the Punjab region to the west.

Now, the few digital breadcrumbs had led to this rural region northwest of New Delhi, the remoteness feeling like they had ventured to a stepping-off point of a world far removed from the ultra-modern cities to the south.

The man tucked his keys into his pocket then adjusted the Glock 19 pistol in his beltline under his baggy shirt.

"See you all soon," he said to his second-in-command on the other end of his earpiece. "The helo will be inbound after that, then we'll be over the border into Pakistan."

"Then the *fun* begins," said the younger man.

The mercenary cinched his shoulder straps, eyeing the bustling crowd on the sidewalk ahead. "At least for our guest."

11

THE SMALL CAFÉ adjacent to the tour bus lobby had already filled with patrons wanting to get their last dose of caffeine and packaged Danishes before departing on the four-hour bus tour of the Kalagarth Tiger Preserve.

Shepard sat at the back of the narrow room, the pedestal-like table little more than a crudely cut piece of round plywood screwed to an old fence post that was bolted to the floor. The wall was covered with faded photographs suspended in cracked wooden frames, showing legendary Indian kings and baronets followed by mustachioed officers in British uniforms, the juxtaposition of both types of images a linear illustration of the muddled politics and colonial occupation of the country.

He took another sip of tepid black coffee then finished off the berry pastry that he was certain had spent most of its early years in a vending machine.

Shepard had arrived early after picking up his paper ticket next door for the 8 a.m. tour departing in fifteen minutes. His eyes had never left the front door, scanning the thirteen other participants who had signed on for the eco-tour. Earlier, he had lingered near the ticket venue for a few minutes, glancing at the computer screen behind the counter at the names of the other travelers, most of whom were listed as hailing from Israel, Great Britain, Japan and America.

As each person got in line to place their coffee order, Cal's attention shifted to the four Anglos sitting at tables in the corner near the entrance. Three men and one woman. The pasty-faced trio looked like they were old friends by their camaraderie and laughter, while the woman kept her gaze fixed on a guidebook on local wildlife, her eyes often scanning over the top of her book at whomever walked inside the front door.

To their left was a young Israeli man who seemed more interested in the woman's tan legs than his own wife, who was busy texting. Next to them was a forty-something man wearing sunglasses and a brimmed hat pulled down low on his forehead. He was sipping his Darjeeling tea while keeping his gaze fixed on the pedestrians on the sidewalk.

Shepard finished his coffee, sliding his chair back away from the older Asian couple to his left, who were close enough that he could smell the man's piercing aftershave.

He wondered if the tight confines of the café were designed to prepare them for the claustrophobic experience of being in the antiquated tour bus he'd seen parked out back.

He glanced down at the incoming number on his vibrating iPhone.

"Go ahead." He slid his chair back further away from the other tourists.

"Have you ID'd Zemenova yet?" said Viper. Shepard was

surprised at the clarity of her voice given that she was 1,600 miles to the south in Mumbai.

"Not yet, but I have a few ideas. I saw that there were several women on the travel roster for the tour company, and that's the only way for civilians to enter the tiger reserve north of here. That's where the other landline phone number is located that showed up on that list I obtained from the comms facility."

"I'll see what I can turn up on the security cameras in the town you're in, though I'm not hopeful since there are only three."

"You sound tired. Didn't you get any rest last night?"

"Still a little hung-over from my trip. My ears haven't adjusted from changing elevations multiple times in shitty single-engine planes on the way back from Bulgaria."

"But you got what we needed, right?"

"Of course, or I wouldn't have come back this early. Geez, Cal, have a little faith."

He sighed, leaning back and lowering his voice. "Sorry, you're right. I'm just ready for this shit to be over. I'm ready for this treasure hunt around India to be done. And I know this can't be fun for you and the guys either."

He could hear her feverishly typing on her laptop as she continued breaking the encryption on the local security feeds. "I told you before that I was good to go with whatever was needed to bring all of this to a close."

"Let's hope convincing her to work with us will be easier than tracking her down." He scratched the side of his black beard while lowering his voice. "Burke only mentioned that she was a colleague, so I'm assuming they were on good terms, but if she had a hand in his software development, then she's probably been trying to stay off the radar because of what happened to him."

"Why wouldn't she have left India by now then? We've tracked her to three cities in this country since we've been here. There must be someone or something that's causing her to stay."

"Yeah, and why would that landline number I tracked down lead to this jungle tourist trap? It'd be much easier to disappear in a big city."

He scanned a young couple who had just walked in, wealthy Filipinos by the looks of their attire.

"And what are your plans when this is all over? Still going to look into private security for wealthy Euro-billionaires?"

"Hell, yeah. For what I could make in three months escorting former ambassadors and their families around the world, I could retire when I'm forty."

"So next year."

"Shut up, jackass. I've got another decade to go."

"That's what you keep sayin' anyway."

"You sure know how to talk it up with a lady."

"I used to," he whispered in a barely audible voice.

"Sorry, Cal, I didn't mean to..."

"Don't sweat it."

Cal felt his heart sink, reflecting back to the last time he'd joked with his wife Cassie.

In another world far from these shores.

When life held such promise and hope.

"You still there?" Viper said, her typing ceasing. "I'm not turning up anything on the cameras in that little one-cow town you're in, but maybe Zemenova has already staked out the security cams to avoid scrutiny, especially given how well she's eluded being recorded in Mumbai and the other cities we've tracked her in."

He slid his chair further to the right after the older

couple left upon hearing the tour bus driver announce it was boarding time.

"I've gotta go for my Disney ride through the jungle, and there's probably little reception where we are headed, so I'll be in touch later."

He stood up, arching his back as he stretched. "Hey, I just want you to know that whatever the outcome of this next week, I am eternally grateful for all you've done and for sticking it out with me for so long. I'm gonna owe you big time after this."

"Hell, you have gone the distance for me more than once, Cal, but who's counting, right." He could almost hear her smug grin through the phone, which was quickly replaced by a startled tone.

"Well, well...so I did manage to find something that looks of interest. There's an old payphone outside of a little market three blocks from your location. It's the same land-line number that you tracked down from that comms facility. A young Anglo woman was there just a few hours ago."

"Making a call?"

"Negative. She actually slowed down as she walked near it like she was expecting it to ring. She was clearly speaking to someone for a minute then hung up and turned around, heading from the direction she'd just come. I'll send a photo of her over in a second."

"Sounds like an old-school type of audio dead-drop. If this is Zemenova, then she knows a few tricks beyond the cyber world."

"Agreed."

His phone buzzed, an image of the individual at the pay phone appearing on the screen.

Shepard glanced at it then up at the young woman at the corner table who had lingered longer than the others. She got up, leaving her guidebook on the table as she exited the café, heading towards the bus.

He put on his sunglasses, casually strolling out the front door like he was a carefree tourist about to embark upon a jungle adventure, hoping that was all the day would bring, but his gut feeling warned him otherwise.

12

WEST BALTIMORE

AFTER THE DRIVE back from doing the recon on Begley's facility, Nolan pulled off the interstate, taking a meandering route through the west end of Baltimore before making his way down a two-lane secondary highway for four miles. Turning right onto a narrow road that felt like it contained all of the city's potholes, he continued south for one mile, stopping before a twelve-foot-high gate that automatically swung open as he approached.

He headed inside the parking lot, which was overgrown with weeds jutting from the cracks in the fractured asphalt, then drove towards a cluster of eight buildings in what was once a large cement production facility.

Pulling into an open Quonset hut, he parked beside four other vehicles, the steel double-doors of the structure closing as he exited his vehicle and walked towards a stairwell in the northeast corner.

Descending two floors, he tapped in the six-digit

numeric code on the keypad by the vault-like door, heading inside once it hissed open.

Nolan stowed the Pelican case with the audio surveillance equipment amongst the other disarrayed items on his makeshift desk then headed past the six intel staff at their workstations, grabbing a leathery, day-old donut off a plate before venturing towards the heart of Foley's operation, which was little more than two large sections of plywood suspended over blue barrels.

Surrounding this command station were a half-dozen whiteboards covered with maps and photographs, with Foley's chief cyber expert Kyle West's desk occupying the rest of the workspace.

The colonel's crack unit of intel analysts and field operators was comprised of only sixteen people, pulled from JSOC, CIA or the NSA and vetted entirely by Foley. There were no references or recommendations to be had; he only chose operators and intel analysts he knew personally from the past three decades of working in the special-forces and black-ops world.

These were men and women at the upper echelons of their tradecraft, who had repeatedly demonstrated their valor under fire and whose commitment to serving their country outweighed the inherent risks of operating in the precarious world of clandestine ops.

For Nolan, who had been approached three months ago by Foley after completing his last mission with Operational Detachment Delta, he was experiencing an operator's wet dream given the colonel's legendary reputation in the spec-ops community and his unwavering devotion to his team members.

Nolan was pretty sure that Foley hadn't even finished his pitch before he found his hand extended, ready to sign on.

The operational tempo within the new team was beyond anything he had experience in his fourteen years of service with the army, and the seemingly effortless way Foley had of enabling a crew of alpha dogs to gel together was impressive.

Adding to this were the computer capabilities, which Foley indicated were in their infancy, awaiting a promised piece of critical software that would transform their intel-gathering abilities to a level never before seen within U.S. agencies.

The latter was beyond Nolan's experience, but he could tell by the gravity of Foley's words, West's unrelenting computer work, and the enigmatic involvement of Shepard in India that an epic battle for the soul of America was being played out, and the rights of its citizens were at stake. There was no place else on Earth that he would rather be right now.

Nolan stood opposite Foley and West, who were both poring over the satellite images of the Arlington medical building that Begley had been seen entering earlier.

"There's no question. According to this, there are clearly twenty-one floors," said Foley.

"That topmost floor is listed as being owned by a company called Corey Logistics," said West. "The only paperwork on them is what they filed when becoming a corporation, almost five years ago. But here's the funny thing —when I looked up the history of that building, it appears that it was originally built in the '70s as a private psychiatric hospital then closed down about nine years ago, sitting vacant until last year, when the place was renovated and turned into the current facility, which is largely leased medical offices."

"But with its own designated elevator shaft that only

goes from the back of the building by the parking lot to that one floor," said Nolan.

"That was actually the service elevator from when it was a hospital," said West. "Clearly, it was left intact and updated when Begley moved in, which would keep it off the radar of the other civilian personnel in that building."

Foley glanced over at the schematics on West's computer screen. "Without any eyes or ears in there, it's going to be hard to figure out what he's doing. Could be a SCIF site or a detainment center for all we know."

"I've examined the electrical output that's being piped to that floor, and it's on par with what I've observed with large computer software firms. It's actually similar to our output here," said West.

"Why would he have an off-the-books cyber group there when he already has access to all of the intel agencies in this country?" said Nolan.

Foley rubbed the back of his neck. "I've known Begley since he came up in D.C., mainly in his role as director of national intelligence. He's indicated in past meetings on the Hill that the Patriot Act is too weak and that a more focused program needs to be in place for monitoring U.S. citizens. I remember once after a meeting, he made an offhand remark about 'Americans needing to be protected from having too much freedom.' It's his personal mission in life to boost the capabilities of domestic surveillance in this country, but based on his own interpretation of what he considers a threat."

He glanced at the former Delta operator. "If I had to guess, I'd say that the Magellan program you overheard him and the senator talking about is what he's got underway in that building. But where the hell is he getting his funding from?"

Nolan shook his head. "You told me before that he also had access to an older version of the Perseus program. If he's using that to enhance his own cyber creation, then a domestic surveillance system would be within easy reach for him and his staff."

"His version would be a month or two less developed prototype than what we have." Foley thrust his chin towards the large array of mainframes in the warehouse. "This is the most up-to-date version of Perseus that exists, secured by Neil Patterson immediately after the assault on Burke's estate that claimed so many lives." He gave a pained expression, glancing at Shepard's name listed in red marker on the whiteboard. "But without the goddam source code, Perseus is only going to be an amped-up super-computer."

"Such a super-computer, even if a lesser gen than ours here, would still provide Begley with considerable reach in domestic surveillance," said West. "If we can get that source code integrated properly into Perseus' rightful mainframes here, then we will be able to use its unique detection capabilities to pinpoint any sociopolitical anomalies related to this Magellan device of his."

Foley walked around the table, stopping before a photo of Begley taped on the whiteboard to his left. "With him due to leave office soon, I think he's been greasing the wheels on this Magellan project so that he can reap the benefits of it once he's in the civilian sector. That means someone up high in the Senate would have to sign off on it. If Begley's got a domestic surveillance system about to launch and it's off the books here on our own soil, then knowing the unscrupulous prick he is makes me think he's got his own little network within our government working to support his agenda."

West scrolled through some antiquated blueprints,

pausing at an electrical diagram. "Years ago, I worked as chief security officer for a Fortune 500 company before coming to work for the NSA. One of our clients was a large utility company that covered all of New England. One thing we were always concerned about was someone hacking into their energy grid and causing a massive blackout. Those types of gaping holes in cyber security have since been patched throughout much of the industry, but the weak link with some companies, especially private ones, is with the protective relays. These relays prevent overloads to circuit breakers and disconnect critical hardware in the event of a catastrophic fire or city-wide electrical failure."

"Nice history lesson," quipped Nolan. "You wanna get to the damn point?"

West used his hands to drum-roll on his legs. "Begley's operation must be dependent on a privately controlled power firm so he has exclusive control for his little shadow-op. That might be a system that can be used to literally pull the plug on his cyber-network, but so far, I haven't been able to locate a damn thing on it, if in fact it does exist."

"Not bad, nerd. Now draw up your attack plans and get back to us. It would certainly be a less lethal way into that facility," Nolan said.

"Kyle and I have already been over that end of things and are working on a contingency plan for such an event, but what can you tell me about how hardened the defenses are in that building?" said Foley.

Nolan stared down at the blueprints. "With Begley's connections in the black-ops world, he's probably got that floor protected by a half-dozen mercs and some cutting-edge visual security feeds embedded in the elevator shaft, roof and egress routes, so it would take a Herculean effort to breach that place."

"I figured as much. Given our time constraints, I'm not signing off on any Red Cell ops to break into that facility, and we need to uncover more about this proposed attack by the Sentinel group you mentioned," said Foley. He glanced over at the athletic figure of Melissa Hamill, the blonde-haired female analyst in the next room who had worked in Eastern European field-ops for years.

"But the use of other assets to gain access to Begley and his outfit is not out of the question."

13

CAL PUSHED past a flock of chickens on the sidewalk, making his way around the back of the tourist trinket shops to the rear parking lot. He stepped up into the old bus, hearing what he thought were the vehicle springs creaking from the movement. He took a seat at the back, his button-up shirt already sticking to the cracked leather seats from the humidity and stagnant air.

He swiveled his hips slightly to prevent the concealed HK pistol at his four o'clock digging into his side as he watched the other patrons who were boarding. His eyes casually floated across the thirty-something woman with blonde hair from the coffee shop whom Viper had helped him identify.

Her facial features appeared European. Her hands were deeply tanned and the nails short and slightly chipped.

Unusual for someone who was supposed to be glued to a keyboard as a computer coder. Is this really Terry Zemenova?

She was dressed more like a local than a tourist, with faded jeans, a green Henley t-shirt and weathered hiking boots. Even her fraying brimmed hat looked like it had spent a few seasons in the elements.

Cal could tell by her subtle but frequent head movements that she was relying on her peripheral vision to observe movement amongst the other passengers and in the aisle behind her, but he didn't think that she had made him.

A part of Shepard felt like making a beeline for her, spilling out his connection to Burke and his reasons for being here now, but something was amiss, and he needed to assess the situation—assess *her*—further before a move was made.

The skinny driver climbed on board, standing in the middle of the aisle. His toothy grin was accentuated by his deeply furrowed skin that resembled the leather on an old mitt. He spoke with a thick accent and choppy English as he glanced around at the eager tourists.

"I am Abhay. I will be guide for next four hours while we drive through tiger preserve. You will see amazing sights. I will make frequent stops so you can photograph wildlife, but please stay in bus all times unless we are at viewing area." He motioned to the armrests. "There are water bottles in your cup holders, so get plenty. Today will be near 38 degrees." He paused and smiled at a light-skinned couple up front. "Or 102 degrees for those from America."

The driver finished his canned speech and was about to close the door when he paused, watching a tall European-looking male enter the bus. He handed his ticket to the driver then sauntered down the aisle, gazing at the other passengers before sitting in a vacant seat at the midpoint.

Cal glanced at the man, who sat with his gaze alternating between the travel brochure in his hands and the view out the front window as the driver lurched the bus forward.

The lanky European was clad in safari shorts and a neatly pressed shirt that looked like it had just been plucked off the racks of an outdoor store in New Delhi. But it was his cracked leather boots that stood out to Cal. They were full-length and more akin to the type of footwear he'd seen with the Danish military.

Despite the seemingly exhilarating atmosphere permeating the air from the other tourists, it didn't take more than a second for Cal to realize a familiar gut feeling was emerging, connected with a predator much different than the jungle cats at their destination.

14

THE MERCENARY HAD DONE a hasty examination of the other passengers before settling into his seat, trying his best to relax his shoulders and feign a smile but only managing a plastic grin.

Either way, it wouldn't matter. He had already ID'd his target. Now, all he had to do was wait for the coming choke-point in the jungle road thirty minutes from now.

Soon, he would wrap up this chase and be collecting his final payment before leaving this squalid country.

He glanced at his watch, counting down the kilometers on his GPS and pacing his breathing for the coming apprehension of a long-awaited prey.

15

THERESA ZEMENOVA HAD KEPT a watchful eye on the bearded man at the rear of the bus. It was with some uncertainty that she tried to determine if he was the same man she'd caught a fleeting glimpse of during her hasty exodus from Mumbai three weeks ago.

At the time, she had thought her paranoia at being discovered in India was getting the best of her, but now she knew that such instinctive reactions were what had kept her alive for so long in this country and her former homeland.

It was only the security system she had surreptitiously installed in the hallway leading up to her small apartment in Mumbai that had alerted her to the intruder, but the facial recognition program on her laptop had come up blank on the man's identity.

How could they have found me? I've been meticulous in covering my tracks and staying under the radar. God, this can't be happening. First, Stephen Burke's death last month, and now someone is on my trail.

She glanced nervously at the dirt road ahead, knowing they would be inside the 74,000-acre jungle preserve within minutes. Then she would be able to break away from the group at the first stop and head on foot towards the northern perimeter where an old friend was waiting.

She breathed a sigh of relief, recalling memories of the tranquil preserve ahead, but it was short-lived, as the bus suddenly slowed, the driver nervously looking at the vehicle in a bend in the road fifty yards distant.

Theresa leaned forward, her eyes widening at the group of five men climbing out of the Land Rover with pistols in their hands. She felt her heart punching against her ribs, and she slowly swiveled to glance back at the bearded man in the rear of the bus who had just stood up and begun moving towards her.

16

SHEPARD SAW the latecomer lean forward in his seat, reaching for something under his shirt, his eyes fixed firmly on the blonde-haired woman two seats up from him.

Cal alternated his gaze between the profusely sweating guy and the approaching cluster of armed men who had just come into sight down the road.

He turned around, unlatching the rear emergency exit and scanning the road behind the bus to make sure no one else was approaching, then he bolted up, rushing towards the man, who had just shouted something in Russian at the blonde woman, his Glock now visibly pointing at her as he shoved her back down into her seat.

The shouts of the other passengers frantically trying to pour out the front door cloaked the thumping of Cal's boots, but the man spun towards him at the last moment, leveling his pistol.

Shepard rushed in, jamming the weapon hand against the man's stomach then driving a vicious head-butt into the gunman's face.

The remaining people around him began flooding into the aisle, shrieking as they rushed for the front exit, ploughing past Shepard, whose grip was torn away from the man's Glock.

Cal was now being pulled along by the river of panicked tourists. The gunman raised his weapon, aiming it at Shepard's chest. A gunshot rang out, and an older woman who passed in front of Cal took a round between the shoulder blades, collapsing onto him. He slid to the floor with the limp figure.

The frantic herd was nearly out the door, and Cal could hear more gunfire outside as he fought to shove the dead woman off him while removing his own pistol. From his hip, he squeezed off three rounds, one grazing the retreating mercenary in the right arm while the other two struck him in the mid-back. The man fired wildly into the bus as he ran, kicking open the rear emergency exit and diving out.

Cal stood up, seeing the blonde-haired woman leaning out from her scrunched position in her seat and checking the pulse on the lady splayed on the floor as more gunfire rang out from the front of the bus. Cal peered above the seats, seeing the advancing gunmen methodically mowing down the other tourists who were trying to run down the road or into the jungle.

He was shocked to see the young woman still in the bus, wondering why she hadn't fled with the rest, but he didn't have time for questions.

"We need to go. I'm guessing those guys are here for you by the way Mr. Friendly back there was eyeing you during the drive."

She gave him a pensive nod, her eyes darting between the two exits.

Cal stood in a partial crouch, heading towards the rear,

seeing the lone gunman lying immobile on the ground. It was only blind luck from glancing back over his shoulder that enabled Cal to escape being bludgeoned by a fire extinguisher racing towards his skull, a wild look overtaking the woman's eyes. He sidestepped, the full force of the object impacting the top of the padded seat. He shoved the woman back into the aisle, grabbing her throat as she started clawing at his arm.

"Stop, that hurts! I'm not here to harm you."

"Who the hell are you?" she said with a slight accent.

At his next words, she stopped resisting. "A friend of Stephen Burke's, and right now, I need you to follow me."

She slowly sat up then followed him to the exit. Cal leaned back, grabbing the fire extinguisher that had nearly split open his skull, then hopped out the door. The gunfire at the other end had diminished, which he knew wasn't a good thing for the doomed tourists.

"I'm going to create a distraction, then we're gonna head into the jungle."

She moved up behind him, bending over to retrieve the Glock from the slumped figure on the ground.

"You know how to use that?" he said, noticing her trigger finger resting on the slide.

"Yes, I have some experience."

"Just make sure to keep that barrel pointed down at the ground when we're on the run." He heard the crunching of gravel from the other gunmen moving towards the front of the bus.

Shepard leaned out, flinging the fire extinguisher onto the road beyond the front bumper of the bus then squeezing off a 9mm round. The resulting explosion sent pressurized metal shrapnel into the group of five men.

Cal darted out, shooting one figure in the head as he

staggered along the shoulder of the road then bolting into the jungle as the woman followed behind him.

17

THE MERCENARY STRUGGLED to his knees, coughing as his mid-back throbbed savagely from the two hollowpoint rounds that had struck the Kevlar plates under his reinforced photographer's vest.

"You good, Victor?" said his second-in-command, Yuri, who helped him to his feet.

The man swore in Russian, referencing the mysterious shooter who had surprised him. He glanced around at the splayed bodies of bullet-riddled tourists along the side of the road. "Where the hell is the woman?"

Yuri waved his Glock towards a faint animal trail in the jungle that disappeared down a heavily treed slope. "They're only a few minutes ahead of us. That bearded guy with the woman dropped one of our guys with a single shot to the head...while he was running."

"Looks like there's another interested party apart from our employer, only that hitter had some advanced combative skills." Victor remove the yellow bandanna about his neck, wrapping it around the bullet graze on his left arm.

The three other remaining men moved up, reloading

their pistols then slinging their backpacks into position. Yuri removed his spare Glock, handing it to Victor, who racked the slide then slid the weapon into his concealed holster.

He grabbed Yuri's arm, shoving him towards the Land Rover. "Drag these bodies off the road and ditch the bus, then I want you to head north and wait by the park perimeter near the lodges. I'll head to the other location with the rest of the men. There are only two outposts in this entire place, and all the trails eventually lead to those locations."

Victor grabbed a water bottle from Yuri's pack, gulping it down then pouring the rest over his flushed face. "And remember, we need the woman alive, but that piece of shit with her...wound him then leave him for the tigers."

18

Langley

Virginia

WHEN THE ELEVATOR doors slid open on sub-level three, Lynn Vogel was met with startled expressions as she walked by colleagues and guards whose customary greetings were replaced with cursory nods.

She glanced down at her white blouse and blue skirt, wondering if there was something amiss with her outfit, then pushed on towards the security access door that led to the tactical-operations wing for the search-and-destroy unit's Intel division.

Swiping her keycard, she entered another passageway that led past a rectangular briefing room on the right and the massive control center on the left where her team of eleven analysts were overseeing and assisting with operations abroad.

Heading to her office, Lynn stopped by the large observation window of the control center, gazing around the room. Upon seeing her, several of the staff whispered to each other then nodded at their colleagues, who swiveled around to see their boss.

What the hell is going on?

She swung open the door and boldly entered, putting her hands on her hips as she looked at Rebecca, the assistant analyst on her left.

"Is there something I should know about?"

The redheaded woman hopped up, brushing her hands along the sides of her skirt as if she was being interviewed. Rebecca's eyes darted towards Vogel's office door.

"He's been waiting for a while, and he seems pretty... uhm...pissed off. He was in here for a while talking to a few of us about the work we do."

"Who?"

"Director of National Intelligence Jason Begley. I thought you knew he was here."

Shit. He's never come to visit me. Is he going to slash our budget and personnel before he leaves office next week? That bastard's never been a fan of field-ops.

Vogel pivoted slightly, looking behind her as if she was a surfer who had just heard a tsunami warning. She turned towards her staff, emitting a weak smile. "Continue with your work. The director is probably just here to discuss his incoming replacement. Nothing to worry about."

She left the room, her gait less steady than when she entered. Standing before her office door, she gripped the silver handle, taking a deep breath then heading inside.

She only took a few steps forward before planting her feet. Begley was actually sitting in her seat, his gaze focused downward on some documents on her desk. On either side of him were two burly members of his security detail.

The nerve of this guy, sitting in my seat and rifling through my case files.

She cleared her throat. "Director Begley. This is quite a surprise. How may I help you?"

He leaned back, removing his reading glasses and casually flinging them on the desk. Begley motioned to the chair across from him. "Please sit. Let's you and I have a talk."

She remained still, folding her arms. "About?"

"You worked for a few years under Neil Patterson, overseeing his search-and-destroy units, didn't you?"

"Is that a question, sir? After all, you know that's all we do in this division."

"And you were good friends with Agent Shepard too, as I understand it. The same man who betrayed his country and this agency and most likely fled these shores with some proprietary government software that wasn't his."

"Shepard was one of the finest agents the CIA ever had, and your claims are...well, sir...not a reflection of reality."

Begley leaned forward, resting his hands on the desk and interlacing his fingers. He glanced up at the hulking bodyguard to his right. "Did she just call me a liar?" Begley shook his head, returning his gaze to Vogel. "Did you just call the director of *all* the clandestine agencies a liar?"

"I said your statements didn't reflect the reality of what happened to Shepard."

"Shepard's a traitorous son of a bitch and will face justice in a courtroom or elsewhere. But your life doesn't have to take a similar turn." He stood up, walking towards her and stopping a few inches from her face. "I've got intel that indicates you recently assisted him with breaching a government comms center in Northwest India."

"What? What on Earth are you talking about? I haven't heard from him since he worked for the agency." She wanted to drive her fist into the man's scrawny jaw. As if sensing her intentions, the two bodyguards moved closer, one standing beside her.

She was enraged at Begley's accusation but also elated that Shepard was still alive, hoping the latter comment about his location abroad wasn't also a fabrication.

"Oh, Lynn, you have had quite an impressive career. It's a shame that Shepard is going to bring it down in flames." He walked to the wall, waving at the framed awards and commendations. "Too bad you'll be known as the agency analyst who assisted America's Most Wanted and is spending her days staring through iron bars at the Supermax."

Her eyes became slits. "Anyone who knows me and works with me will tell you that my record is spotless, so whatever bogus claims you've constructed, thinking you could blackmail me in some fashion to take a fall for you... well, sir, you can rot in hell."

She put her hands on her hips, taking a step towards him, causing him to back up slightly. "That's what this is, after all, isn't it? I don't see an agency lawyer and a case officer here, per protocol with such outlandish accusations, so what is the game you are playing, *sir*?"

"Foley and Shepard. I want everything you have on them and their locations or I will burn your career—your world —to the ground." He looked beyond her out the window at the other analysts. "And maybe even a few of your staff will come along as collateral damage."

She pulled her shoulders back. "You've got nothing on me, and your claims are all fabricated. I'd like to see an agency lawyer now."

He sighed, leisurely walking along the bookcases along the other wall. Begley picked up a framed photograph that showed Vogel next to a woman a few years younger than her and a small boy.

"I hoped it wouldn't come to this, Lynn, but you've forced my hand. There is simply too much at stake."

He held up the photo. "It's Lara, isn't it...your kid sister and her son, Tyler?" He looked at the blond-haired bodyguard next to him. "Weren't they at the park near Main Street this morning? Or was that yesterday?"

"This morning from 10-12," said the man in a monotone voice.

Vogel went to lunge forward, her fist leaving its coiled position. The bodyguard held up one hand, grabbing her wrist and shoving her back. "Easy, miss, I don't want to hurt you."

She yanked her hand free, her face burning red. "But you'll let your boss hurt my sister and her son?"

"Oh, stop, it doesn't have to come to that," said Begley, handing the photo to her. "None of this has to happen if you will work with me."

Vogel wanted to throat-punch the bastard, but she knew he could follow through on everything he'd said. His reach in the intelligence community and in D.C. was far too great to form a defense against him given her limited position at the agency. She thought of the irony of her role—the power she held in being able to track, dissect and ensnare an enemy combatant's life abroad, but now she was so helpless against the despicable predator before her.

If Foley and Shepard are involved in something, it must be significant enough to pose a direct threat to Begley, probably not anything related to the well-being of our country, knowing what a self-serving thug he is.

Vogel glared at him then clutched the photo against her chest. "I haven't had contact with either Shepard or Foley in almost two months, but you must already know that given your access to NSA feeds and your other agencies."

Begley smiled, sitting on the edge of her desk. "You are the pride and joy of the Search and Destroy division, Lynn. With your reputation as the chief targeter here, I'm sure you will be able to apply your considerable skills in locating them and in making certain that Shepard can't duck under the radar again."

"With your access to the intel agencies under your command, it seems to me that you would have located them already. What makes you think I can?"

"Few people at Langley have the capabilities and intel experience to do what you do. Plus, you know them like few others, both personally and operationally...and Shepard trusted you. That may be all the edge I need in locating him."

She looked out the window at her other staff in the tac-ops center, her stomach growing queasy. "And how do I explain that we are using our resources for targeting two former agents, and, in the case of Foley, someone who could be on U.S. soil?"

"I'll take care of the paperwork and fine print, but stress to your team of analysts that this stays in-house. Not a word of this to the agency director here."

The blond-haired bodyguard handed her a cellphone. "For keeping Director Begley updated on your efforts."

The men walked to the door, and Begley paused before opening it. "And Lynn, bear in mind that you will be under constant surveillance, digitally and in every other manner of your daily life, so don't try to contact anyone or warn your sister. That would end very badly, trust me."

She watched the door close in slow motion, her world constricting around her. She felt like vomiting, her legs growing shaky.

Vogel shuffled to her desk, slumping into the chair, her grip on the photo tightening with each labored breath.

19

CAL FELT the wet smack of another palm branch in his face as they trotted along the narrow deer trail below the base of the grassy slope. The jungle was dense enough at this point that the bullet-ridden battlefield on the road above seemed miles away.

Zemenova followed on his boot heels, the thick humidity drenching her clothes as if it had been raining.

A half-mile later, they paused beside the trunk of a large banyan tree, Cal scanning the route they'd just taken but only catching glimpses of bright red birds flitting through the canopy.

"So, how did you know Stephen Burke exactly?"

"I could ask you the same thing," she said, her English less pronounced.

"Your accent...Georgian?"

She blew a strand of hair off her nose. "Very astute, Mr. ...?"

"Cal...Cal Shepard."

Her eyes darted along the ground then slowly up at him as she took a step back. "I know that name. You were affiliated with Burke and his research. The news reports online indicated you were responsible for...for the death of him and his staff."

He licked his lower lip, staring up at the faint sliver of cobalt sky piercing through the green foliage. "Did they also mention that I lost my wife in that explosion?"

"I'm sorry, I didn't know. I just remember the day that Stephen died. I was just returning from a trip up this way when I read online about what happened."

"He's why I'm here now—why I've been trying to track down your elusive ass for the past three weeks since fleeing my country. Stephen told me to find you to finish what he started."

"I thought everything of Burke's was lost...his research and designs stolen."

"Not all of it. He left me with an encrypted hard-drive— a heavy-duty military type that he said contains the source code for Perseus. Said you would know what to do with it."

She shook her head. "No, no, this can't be happening. That's how they must have located me in this country."

"Who?"

"Those guys back at the bus—they were Russian mob, the same ones who have been searching for me. That's why I've been on the move for the past few weeks. And if you have the source code in your possession, then that explains how they knew where to find me. They may have been piggybacking off your efforts and data searches about me, connecting the dots on where I was heading."

He thrust his chin down the trail, urging her to push on with him as they continued talking. "Why does the mob have an abduction order out on you, and what does Burke's black box have to do with all of this?"

"That device is unique, partly because of his software

designs but also because of the hard-drive unit itself, which hijacks energy grids whenever it's activated."

He thought back to the unusual power outage at the comms facility. "So, it activates by itself to, what, to replenish its power supply or something?"

"Not exactly. I'm not really sure to be honest, since it sounds like Stephen must have modified the original source code I designed for him so it would infiltrate other computer systems—to what end I don't know. I'll have to take a look at it."

He slowed his gait to hop on rocks across a small creek. "Well, it's back at a safehouse location a few hours away. Once we get out of here, we can head there and piece all of this together."

"I'm sorry, but if the mob is here, then they will eventually track down the signal that the device gives off when it's activated, and I don't want to be anywhere near it when that happens. Plus, I need to get to the north end of the park by nightfall. I have someone meeting me there."

He glanced at the dense jungle then thought about the remoteness of their location. "It looks like your location is already pretty damn obvious to the goons behind us." He stopped on the trail, squaring off with her. "You wanna explain how the hell the Russian mob is connected to Burke's hard-drive?"

She sighed, biting her lower lip. "Because I stole it from them."

20

AT THE BOTTOM of the slope, Victor had to stop and remove the trauma kit from his pack, popping two painkillers for his bruised ribs and back from the two 9mm bludgeons that he'd taken in the bus.

The short henchman to his right pointed to the fresh disturbance in the mud. "Two people's tracks heading this way."

"Just remember, there are also fucking tigers here, lots of them, so keep your eyes open for those kinds of tracks too," said Victor, causing both of his men to shoot longing glances at the road up top.

He needed to find the woman before dusk, when the sole park ranger would be patrolling the outer roads in his jeep and be on the lookout for a missing bus full of tourists once that company reported the party overdue.

By then, we better have that bitch and be at the helo extraction site north of here.

Victor rubbed his sore nose as he silently cursed the bearded man at the back of the bus who had interfered with his plans.

Maybe I'll take you with us and see how you handle gravity from 5,000 feet above the jungle.

21

CAL WASN'T sure what to make of the enigmatic woman and, frankly, without the Langley databases to confirm her identity, he was relying on the string of clues about her that he and Viper had put together since arriving in India along with the information she'd just confirmed about Burke.

Shepard gave the woman a hard stare, still registering the revelation of Perseus' origins. "You're telling me that Burke was working all this time with stolen Russian software?"

"Mmm...that is the simplified version. For starters, the device I stole contained several encrypted software programs, one of which would later become the foundation code for Burke's Perseus program. He overlaid his designs onto that platform so Perseus was uniquely his and would have been something solely proprietary to your government."

He stopped at a faint animal pathway to the right, making some scuff marks in the ground and walking a few feet up the trail then stepping off on some rocks and returning to the main rocky trail they had been on.

"What was that for?" she said.

"Dummy trail to slow them down."

"You've done this kind of thing before, I take it?"

"A few times."

"The stuff online about you...it said you were a CIA agent for years. Was that true?"

"Can't remember."

"By the way you handled yourself back at the bus, I'll take that for a yes. So, are you still working in some capacity for your government—is that why you are in India, to track me down?"

"Does it matter? I found you and here we are. What I'd like to know is how you came to work with Burke and pass off this stolen Russian software to him."

"Can we just skip the interrogation and keep moving?"

Cal was about to continue prodding her when he caught a faint glimpse of motion from the direction they'd just traveled. He turned to watch an immense tiger move onto the trail two hundred yards away.

"Maybe you're right," he said. "Pushing on would definitely be to our advantage."

They watched the big cat meander along the trail, pausing to sniff the air then cutting back into the jungle to the left.

She studied the cat with interest. "That's probably the resident male in the area. He will most likely be continuing on to mark his territory in this region before laying up for a few hours."

He gave her a surprised look. "Learn all that from the guidebook back in town?"

"I, uhm, do a lot of reading, and India is one of the few places left in the world that still has a healthy population of tigers," she said. "The park claims that there are 109 tigers in these parts, so what are the chances that this will be our only sighting?"

"That's reassuring. I can see you're a glass half empty kinda woman."

"My world is about data and hard facts. The reality is that we will probably come across more tigers soon."

"And my reality indicates we will most likely come across more fucking Russians."

They picked up their pace now that the trail had opened into a small meadow, waiting until they had gained some distance from the immense cat before he continued grilling her.

"Just keep talking. Burke—how did you two cross paths?"

"I was a computer coder in Moscow. I eventually worked my way up to doing cyber security for this defense contractor there. For the first few years, I worked on blue-team issues, focusing on cyber defense and averting attacks on critical software and physical infrastructure. Eventually, I was transferred to the other side, working on a red team, handling cyber offense, vulnerability assessments and penetration testing. Years of working cyber defense helped me to understand how a hacker thinks and where the weak links are. Becoming a red-team member allowed me to take all of that and turn it against my fellow blue-team members to probe our company's firewalls and defenses for openings, however small."

"The underlying tactics and mindset for cyber warfare are not too different from fighting a small ground war—study your enemies, live and think like them, then use counter-insurgency strategies to exploit the known chinks in their armor."

"Yes, exactly. And after several years of working in the

industry, some of us attended a digital-defense conference in Istanbul. That's where I met Stephen, who seemed to be light years ahead of the rest of the software industry. He was truly a revolutionary thinker. I spent all of my free time hearing him speak and later met him. We crossed paths a few more times over that year at other conferences and then just kept in touch. He didn't have any contacts in Russia, and...well...he *liked* me."

Cal stopped walking, giving her a stern glance. "The Stephen Burke I knew was a man of integrity. Are you saying that you two..."

"It was nothing like that. I knew he was happily married and, frankly, he was nearly thirty years older than me."

"And very rich."

"Like I said, we were friends, and he became a mentor to me in ways that my colleagues in Moscow could never be. He treated me like a daughter."

"That still doesn't explain how an illicit hard-drive from the mob made it from your hands into his."

"About seven years after I met Stephen, I was working for a new contracting firm. We were doing radically advanced cyber offense, but it was all very secretive, and the simulations were done only within our controlled little group of researchers."

She stopped to readjust her ponytail and wipe her sweat-drenched face. "At that time, I was also doing some... how do you say in English...moonlighting with another job after hours."

"In your line of work, that usually means working on the dark web, is that it?"

She flared her eyebrows, continuing. "There was word within one of the groups I did freelancing for that an anonymous Russian oligarch was about to get his hands on cyber-intrusion software. By the language and terms that were being used, I could tell it was connected with the research I was doing at the defense firm. When my colleague David and I began quietly looking into it at my company, someone must have found out what we had stumbled upon. That's when we realized that my boss was being financed by the mob not the military."

He came to a stop at the edge of another small stream, turning around towards her, seeing her eyes welling up.

"They came to silence you both," he said matter-of-factly.

She lowered her head, grinding her boot into the pebbles on the sandy trail. "I destroyed the software at the company, but not before making a copy. I got away in time but David, my...my fiancé, was killed that night in a car crash on a bridge. Authorities said it was from a blowout, but cars don't explode into a fireball like that from a fucking flat tire."

Zemenova put her hands on her hips, her lips trembling. "I didn't know where to go, so I spent the next few weeks on the run then decided to reach out to Stephen."

"Knowing him, he probably went the distance for you. It's who he was."

She nodded. "He arranged to get me out of Russia with a new name and identity. The thing is, he didn't even know that I had the stolen source code at that point. He was just there for me...as a friend. No questions asked. It wasn't until I got to India and met with him a month later that I told him everything and offered to give him the hard-drive that would later become Perseus."

Cal stroked his bristly beard, marveling at Burke's

accomplishments and how many people's lives he had helped to shape. He felt a sense of irony in the recognition that the man who saved Zemenova also set things irretrievably into motion with Cal's path that led him to be a hunted fugitive thousands of miles from home.

In that sense, he felt a strange feeling of shared anguish with the woman standing before him, but it only further galvanized his will to be rid of the black box.

IN THE FADING SUNLIGHT, Victor watched a pair of juvenile tigers working their way across the grassy meadow as he and his two men holed up in some waist-high brush a quarter-mile away.

They remained motionless, with Victor only swiveling his binoculars slightly at the treeline beyond the meadow as he watched the silhouettes of the man and woman from the bus trotting on a trail into the dense jungle ahead.

He removed the walkie-talkie from his belt, turning the volume down to its lowest setting then timing his words with the tiger's movements. "The target is heading in the direction of the southeast cabins for the staff. There is only one road in that direction and, most likely, they won't get there until sunrise, so take a position in that quadrant and await my orders."

"Copy that," said the gruff Russian on the other end.

Victor scanned the immediate terrain behind him, his eyes finally settling on a tangle of fallen trees overgrown with vines.

"We will remain here until tomorrow then continue on."

The skinny man kept a watchful eye on the two young

tigers in the distance. "Why not wait until those things move on then use our NVGs and keep pushing forward?"

"Because, between the snakes, spiders and animals, there are a dozen other nasty predators in this jungle, and I plan to end my days with all of my limbs intact."

22

CAL AND ZEMENOVA trekked for another half-mile until the light had faded enough to make discerning the trail difficult. He removed his pack, pulling out a water bottle and consuming most of the warm fluid while studying the forest in either direction.

To the right was a river meandering out of a narrow canyon heavily choked with vegetation. To the left was an immense rock pile and logjams from decades of flash-floods. In the center of it was a U-shaped configuration of van-sized boulders that looked like the only place that would provide ample protection from approaching intruders while allowing them plenty of escape routes around the back.

Assuming a leopard or tiger doesn't think we're on the menu tonight.

"We'll have to stay put until sunrise, and that place looks like our best option," he said, pointing his chin in the direction ahead.

"You mean that cobra den over there. No, thanks. I'd rather keep moving. There's only another three miles or so until we reach the other developed part of the park—at least that's what the brochure indicated."

"Walking through the jungle ain't like walking through the city. Everything takes three times as long out here. Besides, the cobras will be out hunting in the forest and on the trails, not coiled up in a cold rockpile."

"This region is notorious for cobras. Besides, how would you even know? Have you ever seen one?"

"Plenty, in Africa and elsewhere, and the last time was when a guy got nailed by one in Egypt then had his leg turn to blue Jell-O over the next hour."

"That's a nice image, thanks. What was it again that you said you did for a living?"

He frowned, heading towards the boulder field. "Lately, rescuing annoying tourists."

"Fuck off. I didn't ask for your help, and I sure as hell don't want anything to do with that Perseus project."

He scowled, forging ahead into the forest. "You and me both."

AN HOUR AFTER MIDNIGHT, Cal stood up from his squatted position leaning against a smooth rock slab and stretched his back and neck. The breeze wafting down from the canyon had provided some respite from the heat, but it was hardly enough air movement to keep the mosquitos at bay, and he and Zemenova used their rain jackets as large shawls on their heads to help reduce the facial assaults.

During the rare times when Cal dozed off, the bellowing of nearby male tigers reminded him of his place in the food chain and just how insignificant they were in this immense ecosystem.

Out of habit, he kept his pistol in hand, knowing that he and the woman had probably already been in striking distance of a tiger whose hide was thick enough to prevent any significant damage from 9mm rounds.

The woman sat up, adjusting her facial covering and taking an irritated peek at her watch again, as if the hours to sunrise had changed in the past ten minutes since her last glance.

"So, you didn't answer me back there about how you were connected to Burke," she said.

"He and I knew each other from the defense industry. I used to work as a security consultant." His mind struggled to claw through the tangled web of memories from his past life and the false cover story that he and his former boss at the CIA, Neil Patterson, had concocted. Although Zemenova had evidently read the stories in the media about his employment with the CIA, he wasn't going to feed into it.

"I'd say you were more than just a consultant by how you handled that guy in the bus. I worked with a fair number of former Spetsnaz at my last job in Moscow, and you hold yourself like they did—with a quiet confidence but also with the potential for great violence lurking just beneath the surface. It's hard to turn that kind of thing off once it becomes a default mechanism like it usually does with soldiers."

"I'm not a soldier, and I don't work for the U.S. government. I told you, Burke led me here to find you."

They grew still at the nearby roar of a tiger whose deep chuffs echoed off the cliff walls.

"And you have no idea what Burke wanted me to do with the source code? No instructions? The last time I spoke with him was two months before his death when he asked for my help in double-checking some new lines of code for Perseus."

Cal shook his head, fighting back a grin.

"What?" she said, seeing the dim outline of his face in the moonlight.

"The irony of all this—that he built Perseus upon a stolen program out of Moscow and was using you, a Russian cyber expert, to bounce fucking ideas off of as he developed the software for my government."

"Like I said, I only ever got small segments of code to proof. I still don't know what he was developing or what Perseus was intended for."

"But you know what that source code you stole was originally intended for, and it sure as hell wasn't for creating video games."

"The defense firm I was working with specialized in collating surveillance data, similar to what China has already perfected with round-the-clock monitoring of its citizens."

Cal navigated through his mental notes of what he was supposed to reveal about his former work with Burke, then realized that once Zemenova accessed the source code, she would clearly learn what Burke had developed. Plus, he didn't work for the CIA any longer and had no loyalty to an agency that still had a kill order out on him for crimes he hadn't committed.

He looked at the woman, her dark clothes blending into the boulder behind her, making her pale face seem like a spectral apparition floating above the forest floor.

"Perseus was intended to detect anomalies in the social, political and economic fabric of a city or country that might be connected with forthcoming coups, assassinations or unrest. Burke was granted access to public, private and government surveillance feeds and intel that were fed into Perseus to build its detection algorithms." Shepard stopped abruptly, stemming the tide of words as if it would roll over him.

Her eyes darted along the ground then up at Shepard. "It worked, didn't it? What he built worked. Perseus found something. Is that why he was killed?"

Cal took a long time to respond, his voice lowering. "Towards the completion of the program, a week before his death, it, uhm...it discovered several factors and forces colluding in Venezuela, connected with a political coup that was being backed by some powerful individuals back in the U.S. They saw Burke and everyone connected with Perseus as a threat."

He slid his back down along the boulder, coming to rest in a squat again as he stared into the inky forest. "Perseus had done everything we hoped it would—it was an incredible success and one that would have had the ability to reshape our intelligence agencies."

Zemenova sat more upright. She leaned over, resting her hand on his arm. "I'm sorry for all you lost."

He gave a weak nod, sighing. "So, you asked why I'm here. Why I've been searching for you. Because Burke thought it was important enough to provide me with the source code and find *you* so you could finish what he set out to do. I owe it to him and to everyone who died that day to see this through to the end."

"But where is the rest of his work—the mainframes from that program?"

"Look, I just need you to access the black box I have and see what you make of it—to see if there's something that can still come of it or if I've just spent the past month on a scavenger hunt."

"What is scavenger hunt?"

"A scavenger is like a catfish that roams around looking for scraps and..." He shook his head. "Never mind. The point is, will you be able to figure out what to do with it once it's accessed?"

"That will just keep putting a target on my back with my former employer."

"What if I were able to get you to a secure location where the signal would be contained once the device is accessed?"

She rocked her head from side to side. "It would have to be a government or military installation, and from what you've told me, you're not going to be able to just walk into such a place given your status as a fugitive."

"Just leave that part to me. If I can get you to a secure location, can you help with the rest? *Will* you help me finish this?"

She folded her arms across her chest, leaning back and gazing up at the moon. "I am normally not someone who believes in fate and all that bullshit, but it seems like our paths have crossed out here for a reason. Plus, I am indebted to Stephen...so, yes, I will help you for now. But after that, I am gone."

"Fair enough."

He wondered how much of what she had just agreed to was out of the need to survive the ordeal of escaping the Russians and if she was just saying what he wanted to hear. He suspected her admiration and loyalty to Burke was only outweighed by her need to escape from her old employer.

Who can blame her?

Everyone's out for themselves anyway in this godforsaken world. Life is about self-preservation, especially when you're cut off from home and everybody you once loved.

23

DOWNTOWN PHILADELPHIA

NESSA HOFFMAN PULLED her baseball cap lower to hide her face as she stepped off the city bus, heading down the street towards a used bookstore.

She opened the antique oaken door, hearing the bell on the opposite end of the bronze handle rattle as she stepped inside. Nessa gave a polite nod to the older man in spectacles behind the counter then proceeded down the main aisle, veering to the right towards the Current Politics section.

She looked at her phone again to recall the book title listed on an automated text.

Current Theories in Economics

83

She stopped at the end of the aisle, her eyes tracing along the larger volumes at the bottom before settling on the desired book. Nessa glanced down the aisles behind her, seeing no one present, then retrieved the book and casually flipped to page 83. There was a torn index card with a six-digit code written in pencil. She memorized the number then returned the tome.

She meandered around the other sections for a few minutes, feigning interest in a book on time-travel. She recalled seeing several science-fiction movies with her younger brother when they were kids, both of them wishing they were interplanetary travelers able to escape Earth and the misery of living with their alcoholic mother and abusive stepfather. Instead, she started working a part-time job in high school, squirreling away her money to moving out as soon as she turned eighteen, permanently severing ties with the two miscreants she called parents.

Exiting the store, Nessa walked for four blocks, heading down a flight of steps to a microbrewery that had gone out of business. She paused at the metal door, punching in the six-digit code on the keypad.

Even though she had performed this same ritual at different locations around the city on a monthly basis for the past two years, she still felt a sense of giddiness coupled with anxiety upon entering a derelict building where Sentinel held its meetings.

Crossing the threshold, she let her eyes adjust, closing the heavy door behind her. She pulled a small flashlight from her jeans and turned it on, seeing a trail of fresh foot-prints on the dusty floor.

She headed to the back of the empty building, turning right and heading down another flight of stairs. The knock on the door was repeated six times, the same amount of figures on the numeric code. The handle twisted, the door moving inward an inch as a single blue eye scrutinized her before opening the door all the way.

"Come on in, kiddo," said Russ Buchanan, a thirty-something man who always had a crooked grin. He was dressed in his usual baggy shirt, red baseball cap and faded jeans. Buchanan had taken Nessa under his wing since joining Sentinel, and he had a kind-hearted uncle vibe about him that she had always yearned for as a kid.

She was sure Buchanan wasn't his real name, since everyone was required to have aliases and keep their personal and professional backgrounds from their meetings, but she had gleaned little snippets over the years that Russ was a disgruntled city sanitation worker who had grown up in the rough-and-tumble neighborhoods on the East Side. He had a tough-love attitude but always doted on her during their monthly meetings and at undercover political demonstrations down at city hall.

Nessa placed her iPhone in a thick metal box with the others then joined the circle.

"Buses are running late tonight," she said to the eighteen other members of their group who were standing in a half-circle around their leader, James Reynolds, a powerfully built man who towered over the others.

"Not to worry. We were just going over next week's operation downtown," said Reynolds.

"Maybe Russ can fill you in later on what you missed."

Buchanan winked at her, making her grin. She elbowed him back lightly then stood at attention, fixing her gaze on the man who had spearheaded the effort in Philly to expose government corruption. The rumor in the group was that Reynolds had done time in jail on multiple occasions for staging protests against the last mayor, including handcuffing himself to the doors of a youth rehab center that was slated for demolition to provide a new strip mall.

At twenty-two, Nessa was the youngest member of Sentinel, but her desire for justice and keeping politicians accountable was only exceeded by her passion and drive, and she planned to use her forthcoming degree in social work to further Sentinel's causes within a system marred by corruption and in-fighting.

Reynolds held up a small poster board that had a layout of the downtown region. "The current city admin is hoping to divert funds away from a much-needed housing project in the low-income neighborhoods to the south so they can put in a new spur-tunnel off the subway that will benefit the banks and corporations downtown even though they haven't lifted a single finger to donate to this effort. Instead, the mayor and governor have signed off on using taxpayer dollars to fund this absurdity, pulling precious funds away from the homeless shelter."

He waved his hand up in a broad sweeping motion like he was a Sunday preacher. "The plan that is being foisted upon us by the controlling corporations and government whores who support them will blight this city and strip the homeless, the suffering and the under-privileged of the basic necessities of life while the rich just line their pockets."

He shook his head, his face visibly tense. "Unless a drastic paradigm shift occurs, the rights and freedoms of the individual will always take second place to the needs of the State. Despite my best efforts at anonymously working with the media on exposing our local government's corruption, we need to step up and take things to the next level. A physical statement needs to be made that no one can ignore, and Sentinel will be there to expose these criminals in suits down at city hall."

Nessa felt her heart flutter, her stomach roiling slightly, like she was standing at the starting line on a collegiate track, ready to burst out in a sprint. This was why she had joined Sentinel and gone through the lengthy vetting process to assure Reynolds and the others that she was committed to their cause. To keep those in power accountable and to ensure that those without a voice would have one.

Other groups she'd joined on campus at Temple University were all about well-intentioned rhetoric, membership dues and endless committee meetings that led to little or no change.

With Reynolds and his right-hand man, Buchanan, the men had demonstrated repeatedly that real change only came through sacrifice and persistent commitment to a singular cause, even if it occasionally meant stepping outside of the law. Though she didn't condone violence, she wasn't opposed to physical destruction of property to pull back people's blinders on government abuse of power.

As Buchanan said to her once over a cup of coffee in a diner, "Politics is too important a matter to be left to the politicians."

Reynolds looked around at the other faces in the room. "I will text you along the usual lines in the coming days with your groups and locations for next week."

Reynolds folded up the diagram and zipped up his jacket. "See you on the battlefield then."

The mixed-age group began dispersing. Nessa walked up to Buchanan and Reynolds. "What can I do? Or were individual roles already covered?"

"We need the floor swept before we leave," quipped Buchanan.

"Haha, I meant for what's coming."

"I know, kiddo. You're gonna accompany me and Reynolds to the primary site under the subway."

She rubbed her palms together. "Sounds good. Where and when?"

"Like I said, I'll send a message along the usual lines shortly," said Reynolds.

She gave a two-fingered salute. "Alright, see you guys soon then."

The two men watched her leave, waiting for the door to slam.

"She's got spunk, that one," said Reynolds.

"Enough for three people. Wish everyone could be as dedicated as her."

"You gonna be able to get us down into the old service tunnels under the subway like we discussed?"

Buchanan removed a tarnished bronze key on a cord around his neck. "All set, brother. Working for the city has its perks."

Reynolds gave a hearty nod, heading towards the exit. "Then I'll see you in two days."

"And we set loose the Dogs of War—or in the case of where we're going in those old tunnels, the Rats of War. Once we blow that subway project, there are gonna be a thousand rodents swarming over downtown."

Reynolds chuckled. "How will anyone tell them apart from the bankers?"

24

VOGEL HADN'T BEEN HOME in two days, opting to sleep on the couch in her office and getting meals from the cafeteria on the third floor. She had only recruited one of her staff to help with targeting efforts on Foley and Shepard while keeping the other analysts focused on their duties assisting the currently deployed search-and-destroy units.

So far, nothing had turned up on Foley. It was as if the man had dematerialized from the Earth. She'd only seen such a sophisticated level of counter-intelligence a handful of times, and it was usually connected with someone being sheep-dipped into a black-ops program that required utter deniability.

What are you up to, Colonel? Are you working with Cal, or is he running his own personal op?

The encrypted phone that Begley had provide crabbed across her desk. She reluctantly picked it up, her stomach already beginning to churn.

"Tell me you have turned up other locations in India that Shepard frequented."

"I, uhm, have compiled a few things through examining

the intel you provided about recent events in Northwest India accompanied with satellite feeds from the National Reconnaissance Office."

She fought against uttering anything to the man, the words seeming to stick in her throat. "There were six times Shepard showed up along the coastal cities from Mumbai to Kolkata while two were in smaller towns in the tropical highlands in the northern part of the country."

"Fascinating. So, he likes to travel. Surprise me with something actionable."

"There's a woman he is with."

"One of our agents or an old asset?"

"No, I've never seen her before. I picked up an image of her at a payphone yesterday near a town called Dugadda north of New Delhi. That's also not far from where a busload of tourists were reportedly killed."

She heard a labored sigh before Begley replied. "That's quite a fucking intel briefing, Lynn. Since you're the most resourceful analyst within the agency and have access to billion-dollar surveillance capabilities, you've probably unearthed a shitload of data that you're just sitting on right now." He paused, his voice becoming more of a growl. "What's it going to be, Lynn—you going to get with the goddam program, or do I have to send one of my guys to your sister's house tonight to read her and her kid a bedtime story?"

Even though she was sitting, Vogel felt like she was about to topple over. She held one of the most powerful positions in the clandestine agencies, but now she felt like her foot was ensnared in a steel trap that was scything through her flesh and her soul.

Vogel felt queasy, taking a deep breath then gritting her teeth. She leaned forward, pulling up a minimized screen that showed additional intel she'd gathered during her hasty search for Cal and the woman.

"I, uhm, I did a facial scan on the police images of one of the dead men by the bus. He is connected with the Russian mob out of Moscow, the Orlov crime syndicate in particular." She cleared her dry throat, forcing herself to continue. "His phone was still active, so I hacked into the device, and there was a photo of the woman. Her real name appears to be Natasha Kisyelov, a former software engineer from Moscow, but it appears she's been living in India under the name Theresa Zemenova for some time. She was registered on that tour bus yesterday."

"Good girl, Lynn. I knew you were a rockstar. Now, this information supports a theory I've had all along that Shepard may be trying to find a buyer for Perseus' source code, which he must have in his possession. Maybe he plans to use the woman as a conduit to sell the code to the Russians."

She flared her eyebrows. "I'm not sure what this has to do with Perseus. I thought that project folded after Stephen Burke's death? And why would a Russian crime syndicate be hunting her down if Shepard planned to do business with them?"

"Look, this woman is somehow connected to all of this—to Burke, Perseus and Shepard. If the source code gets into someone else's hands, it will present a national security issue on our shores. Find this woman and Shepard."

"I want assurances that my sister and nephew won't be harmed first."

"How's this—you get me what I want and they'll be removed from my shit list, but I want a location within two hours or that deal is revoked."

The phone went silent. Vogel didn't know if she could have even responded given her burning rage.

She balled her fist, taking a deep breath. *This bastard is going to pay. When this is over, there won't be a place on Earth left for him to hide in. I will fucking destroy him.*

She looked around her office, sure that every facet of her daily life was being monitored as Begley indicated it would. Her home was no doubt bugged, her vehicle's Bluetooth and audio, her office, the tac-ops center and her sister's home. Vogel also couldn't rule out the fact that one or more of her staff may have been compromised either through a pay-off or coercion.

The reality of her predicament left her with few alternatives, knowing that once she was done with Begley's dirty work, the man would throw her to the wolves, by revealing she was complicit in Shepard's escape from justice or merely by eliminating her. She could cope with those realities as long as her sister and nephew were left unharmed.

But she also knew that Begley was nothing more than a cutthroat politician who had been warped by the power of his position, and she had no faith he would honor his agreement.

It took considerable effort to restrain herself from turning her targeting skills on Begley himself to learn the scope of his plan and who his other conspirators were, but she couldn't even consider that course of action until her family was out of the crosshairs. Instead, she tempered her growing fury as she sat at her desk, alternating scanning satellite images of Cal's last location with slowly texting a coded message to a former mentor on a burner phone that rested on her leg under the desk, a life-preserver in her rapidly sinking world.

25

AT DAWN, Shepard and the woman resumed travel on the jungle trail, covering three torturous miles along the barely discernible path before the sun had crested the horizon two hours later. Cal held back his frustration at their slow progress. Normally, two able-bodied people could have covered the distance in half that time, but they made dozens of stops whenever they came across fresh tiger scrapes or cat tracks intersecting the trail, constant reminders that he was not the top predator in the region. ·

As they progressed along the faint pathways, he marveled at Zemenova's adept movements, wondering how much time she had actually spent in Mumbai. Despite his initial impression of her as appearing like another out-of-place tourist on the bus, she seemed quite at home in the jungle and moved with ease, like someone not unfamiliar with living in the wilds.

A few minutes later, Shepard saw a large swath of sunlight penetrating the jungle canopy ahead where the trail came to an end at a small patch of open ground. He and

Zemenova slowed their trot, cautiously approaching the trail terminus.

To the right was a rundown plankboard shack with a tin roof. The screen door was flapping against the frame as a warm breeze flooded across the jungle. Beside the shack was an open tool shed with gas cans, a few chainsaws, shovels and other landscaping implements.

To the left was an old jeep with a faded canvas tarp for a covering over the rear seats.

"This is where I'm supposed to meet my friend," said Zemenova.

"The guy who called you on the payphone back in town a couple of times?"

She shot him a surprised glance. "Yeah, he, uhm, lives in New Delhi, retired from the college there, but spends his weekends volunteering out here, doing trail maintenance."

"And what's he got that you risked traveling all the way to such a remote region?"

"Something I can't leave India without."

He knew the woman didn't trust him. Her answers were often guarded, as if everything percolated through a mental filter before she responded to him. He felt like he always had to fill in the blanks and figured she was referring to obtaining new passports.

"So, he's a document forger? I would have thought with your prior connections on the dark web that you could have something forged in no time."

"I rarely venture online. It's how I've managed to stay off the radar for two years...at least until now, no thanks to you and the Russian mob."

Why would a document forger be spending his weekends out in the jungle? The odd assemblage of story elements didn't add up, but for now, he would just play along until they were clear of the park.

Cal did a final visual sweep of the tiny outpost then stepped out, heading towards the shack. Twenty feet in, he paused, staring at the multitude of fresh footprints in the mud followed by blood spatter on the porch steps.

He heard the familiar but sickening sound of an AK-47 slide being racked then saw two men in tank-tops step out from the woodpile on the other side of the jeep.

Cal kept his pistol frozen against his leg, knowing he only had a 50-50 chance of dropping one of the shooters before the others unloaded on him.

"So, we meet at last," said a voice from the shack. A thirty-something Indian man with a head of wiry black hair stepped out on the porch.

The gangly figure sauntered down the steps like he was going for a morning stroll. Three more armed thugs emerged from the shack, and Cal could see the limp body of a dead man lying on the floor inside.

"No, God, no!" wailed Zemenova as she tried to rush up the steps but was shoved back by the leader.

The men swarmed in around them, removing Cal and Zemenova's pistols.

The leader moved forward, speaking with considerable fluency in English. "I believe you already met my younger brother, Adesh, a few hundred miles east of here when you played savior to that convoy of aid workers."

Cal saw a tattooed image of a black cobra on the man's beefy right forearm. The man held up his iPhone, showing a grainy close-up of Shepard's face.

Cal gazed around at his predicament, feeling like the tiger-infested jungle had suddenly become much safer.

26

SAI PATEL TURNED the phone around, staring at the image then shaking his head. "You know, I'm not surprised my idiot brother met such a fate given he had the hat size of a small child. But my father is now requiring me to take over my brother's shit-hole province in addition to my regular duties in this region, and that really pisses me off...and I have you to thank, it seems."

He raised his left hand, snapping his fingers. One of his henchmen moved up next to Sai, handing over a tablet. He turned it around, showing the screen to Shepard. It revealed drone footage of Shepard and Zemenova walking through the jungle. "When we got a report from my contacts within the local police out here about an attack on a bus, I had my people in the region get some eyes out on the land, and I couldn't believe my luck in finding you. You must have a thing for coming to the rescue of women in the jungle."

Shepard didn't respond. Sai turned his attention to the woman. An expression of dread swept over her pale face. "You a part of this guy's network or just a freelancer?"

"Please, I don't have anything to do with whatever is going on between you and the American."

Sai emitted a wolfish grin. "Ah, 'American,' that's interesting. I would have thought maybe a Brit or Dane, by his looks." He took a step closer to Cal. "Now, why would an American be here on my shores, killing my people? Who hired you?"

"There's no pay required to rid the world of shitbags like the men who attacked that convoy of innocent civilians."

Sai shook his head then sent a surprisingly non-telegraphic punch into Shepard's stomach. Cal's knees buckled, shock registering on his face at the rail-thin man's capabilities. He sucked in a deep breath, resting his hands on his knees.

"My brother, shitbag or not, was going to be taking over as one of my father's lieutenants along the Pakistan border, which will now present a setback for our operations there."

He grabbed Shepard's hair, yanking his head up. Sai's eyes drifted across the stoic man's face then over his athletic arms. "You seem like someone who is no stranger to hardship. Regrettably, such things are becoming a rare trait in men today, and I'm sure you could take a fair amount of punishment before you tell me what I want to know." He twisted Shepard's head to the right towards Zemenova as he removed the sheath knife on his belt.

"But a pretty face like that could sway a man to talk, especially given my skill with a blade. And when I'm done, even the slave traders along the border would turn her away."

"Please, stop. I'm not a part of any of this bullshit," said Zemenova. "He and I were on the bus that got attacked yesterday. I barely know him."

Sai moved up to the woman, resting his knife hand by his side. "Attacked by who?"

Shepard canted his head to the left, hearing the hum of a vehicle engine as a muddy green Land Rover with two white men inside came into view. The same vehicle he'd seen yesterday during the bus assault.

And the man in the passenger's seat had just leaned out the window with his MP5.

27

SHEPARD DIDN'T WAIT for the bullets to fly.

He rushed forward, slamming a hammerfist down on Sai's nose, letting it sail through to his lower lip and chin as cartilage and flesh yielded to the vicious blow. The man was caught off guard, his knees wobbling as he slumped against the fuel barrels. Cal grabbed him by the shirt collar, yanking the pistol from the man's belt then kicking him in the chest, the blow sending him into the side of the old jeep.

He squeezed off two rounds into the face of the nearest thug rushing in from the left, then Cal moved diagonally, body-shoving Zemenova behind a row of steel fuel drums.

Swinging his pistol around, he saw a partially toothless goon leveling his AK at him. The man's finger never got to squeeze the trigger as a barrage of rounds from the Russians punched through his back, sending him face-first into the mud. The air filled with staccato bursts of gunfire as the two Russians took up shooting positions behind the rear bumper of the Land Rover thirty yards away while Sai's men began returning fire.

Shepard ducked behind the fuel barrels, darting a hand

out to retrieve the dead man's AK then sidling up next to Zemenova, who was hunched in a ball.

Cal leaned out, shooting one of Sai's men near the woodpile, two rounds slicing through his thoracic region. He slumped back, tumbling down the grassy incline into the creek.

A blur of rounds peppered the jeep to the left where Sai was trying to climb into the driver's side. Shepard leaned on his shoulder, centering the AK's front sight on the man's waistline and squeezing off a single round. The gangster fell back, clutching his stomach as one of his men ran up to his side.

Shepard was about to shoot the henchman when he caught a glimmer of movement in the jungle to the left. Three other white men, one of whom was the Russian merc Cal had battled in the bus, had just run along the trail into the grass and were making their way along the base of the slope behind the woodpile.

"We need to get the hell out of here," he snapped, sliding back, surprised as he felt the absence of Zemenova behind him. He swiveled, seeing her already bolting inside the shack.

"Dammit." Shepard squat-walked to the edge of the fuel drums as the whirring sound of bullets overhead raced past him.

From the corner vantage point of the last barrel, he could see that one of the Russians at the rear of the Land Rover had blood staining his shirt near his left shoulder and was struggling to maintain his shooting arm.

Cal could make out the barking of three, maybe four AKs near the woodpile from Sai's men, who were still engaged with the shooters on the road. But he knew they would soon be overtaken by the other Russians making their way along the grassy slope.

Once Sai's men were gone, they would be at the mercy of the Russian mercs, and by the looks of the thin-walled wood shack, they wouldn't have much cover.

He glanced towards the entrance, seeing Zemenova kneeling beside the dead Indian man inside, gently brushing her fingers along his cheek, then she hopped up, sliding the desk back from the wall and prying open a loose plank from the floor, retrieving a small pouch from below.

She turned, a look of surprise on her face as she saw Cal staring at her, then she darted to the back door, disappearing into the jungle.

Passports, my ass.

He stepped out a few inches, taking aim and shooting the other Russian by the Land Rover, the rounds shattering his clavicle and trachea, sending him flat on his back. Shepard lunged forward, grabbing a small gasoline can near a chainsaw. He flung the red canister towards the weathered jeep just as the other Russians were advancing on Sai's men from the rear.

Cal unleashed a flurry of rounds towards the gas can as he sprinted for the door of the shack, and the resulting explosion engulfed the vehicle.

The intense fireball sent a flurry of limbs and bodies into the treeline as Cal took cover behind an overturned table inside the shack. Shepard scrutinized Zemenova's dead friend on the floor beside him, his furrowed face and calloused hands resembling many of the other weathered Indians in these regions who spent their entire lives out on the land.

His attention snapped back to the conflagration outside after some of the younger palm trees caught aflame, sending a black cloud of smoke swirling into the canopy. Cal could see there was nothing left alive that posed an immediate threat, but he couldn't be sure that the three mercs were out of commission, and he had no plans to stick around and find out.

He remained in a low squat, backing up towards the rear door. Pausing at the entrance, he checked in either direction for movement then leapt out, trotting to the left, his tracks overlapping those of the woman.

Fifteen yards later, he saw some trampled vegetation near the one-lane road.

Edging to the opening, he saw Zemenova standing over the last wounded Russian, who was now sporting a gash in his forehead from where she'd struck him with a shovel. She bent down, removing his pistol and pointing it at his head as he squirmed back against the rear tire. Without hesitating, she fired off three rounds into his chest.

Shepard slowly moved out from his concealed position onto the road, his AK leveled in the direction of the vehicle.

Zemenova swung her body towards him, her trembling hand aiming the Glock at his head. Cal froze, seeing an expression of terror and rage that he had been privy to before in war-torn cities around the globe. He knew the feelings that were flooding over her right now—the hate, the sorrow and the anguish that comes with extinguishing a life in the hopes that it will erase the horrors of the past.

He lowered his weapon, raising an outstretched hand.

"It's over, for now," he said.

Her hand wavered as tears streamed down her flushed cheeks. She flung the weapon aside, staggering back and sitting on the bumper as she pressed her hands to her face.

"Come on," he said, putting his hand on her shoulder.

"Let's get the hell out of here before more of either party shows up."

FROM HIS PERCH on a ridgeline a mile away, Lucas Bishop followed the Land Rover with his binoculars until it exited the park several miles later then disappeared again on a tangle of roads in the jungle.

He removed the iPhone from his pocket, speed-dialing one of the four numbers programmed into the encrypted device.

A second later, he heard Jason Begley's voice on the other end. "Tell me you've got the source code."

"We will shortly. I need you to track a green Land Rover currently leaving the park from the south."

"There are two days left until the conference in Philly, and you don't have the one fucking thing I sent you there for."

"It'll be in my hands soon."

"You sound certain, but that's not enough."

"You were right about Shepard being in play here. He's with a woman. She must be who the Russians were after when they hit a tour bus near the park. I ID'd one of their bodies, and they showed up on the agency's database as being with the Orlov crime syndicate."

"You sure they weren't after Shepard or doing business with him?"

"If they were, he just took out most of them along with a bunch of Indian guys."

He heard his boss seethe out a long exhale. "Look, whatever clusterfuck is unfolding over there, just make sure it results in your next call to me starting with the words, 'I have the fucking source code.' Got it?"

"Just provide me with the satellite coverage and I'll wrap this up."

He turned off his phone, slid it back into his pocket, then resumed scanning the jungle below before glancing over to the five men spread out in the brush to his right and left.

"Once we've tracked Shepard to wherever he's going, we'll move in and snatch him up then apply whatever measures are required to make him give up the source code."

"Why not just intercept him on the road now?" said a black operator to his right.

"If I were him, I wouldn't be carrying a high-value device like that on me. He's probably got it stashed in a safehouse somewhere and could possibly have some copies of it in other locations or with others on his team. We'll let him lead us to it then take him down from there."

"And the woman? How does she figure into this?" said a goateed man who was scanning the terrain below with his scoped AR.

"Not sure, but she could be the other element Begley indicated before—the one connected with the phone calls to that software guy Burke."

The black operator shook his head. "The defense industry dude that Shepard worked with back in Virginia and supposedly killed? Does anybody here really buy that shit...that Shepard was a traitor? I used to know some guys who ran with him when he was in SAD. Doesn't add up that he'd burn everyone he worked with."

"Doesn't matter," said Bishop. "You know the job. Get the sensitive intel off the streets and back to Begley by whatever means necessary."

He flattened a mosquito on his neck. "And from what Begley told me, Shepard worked in SAD for seven years before getting recruited into a secretive unit by Neil Patterson and Ryan Foley. For all we know, he could be running his own little side-op for them."

"Never heard of 'em," said the short man next to Bishop.

"They were old-school guerilla fighters, and Shepard and the rest of them were part of a specialized search-and-destroy unit that had a heavy emphasis on hand-to-hand skills, since Foley was a hardcore martial artist. He trained his teams to hunt down other assassins using guns, knives, poisons...whatever."

"This guy used to be with the agency, like us, and we're just gonna torture the shit out of him to get what we need? That ain't right," said the black man.

"Then I'll make sure to put you on sentry duty outside the room while I handle things," said Bishop, standing up and stowing his binoculars. "Either way, twenty-four hours from now we'll all be heading back to Virginia with what we came here for, with or without painting the streets with blood."

JASON BEGLEY continuously spun his iPhone on the desk, as if it were a compass needle that would indicate the right direction to take.

He leaned forward, grinding his thumb into his temple, hoping to drive away the constant headache.

Who is Shepard working with? Someone from the agency or another intel group?

His gut told him that Foley was involved, but he had no evidence, and the colonel continued to be an elusive ghost.

Either Foley's deep cover on some black-ops mission abroad or he is operating in the States under the radar on this project with Shepard. But if he has the original Perseus program, then why wouldn't Shepard have turned over the source code to him already?

Shepard's presence in India had complicated his efforts, but now, with someone in the agency potentially providing assistance, he knew that he had to tighten his plan and speed up the timeline, ensuring Magellan's future was secure and, most importantly, that the forthcoming attack at the conference in Philadelphia unfolded without any glitches.

If Bishop doesn't obtain the source code soon, it'll be time to take things to the next level.

28

IT SEEMED like weeks since Vogel had felt the sun on her face as she tried to resume her duties as chief targeter for the search-and-destroy units.

She had met Begley's demands and passed on the information about Shepard's last known location in India. The phone the director gave her had remained silent for the past six hours. And her text message to her former boss, Neil Patterson, had gotten through, allowing the former operator to relocate her sister to a secure location in the countryside near Shenandoah.

As for Foley, the man had simply disappeared. Even with her advanced detection skills, she found it impossible to locate a digital, visual or paper trail on the man. That only reaffirmed to her that the colonel had gone dark in a way that was completely off the grid in some isolated location, or he was employing software capabilities beyond even what she commanded at Langley.

She thought back to the disappearance of Perseus' mainframe and all of Burke's tech research nearly two months ago.

Could Foley have been behind that?

She leaned back in her chair, thinking of the tangle of events from that tragic day. *Was Patterson himself involved... maybe both men working on this together?*

In the twenty-four hours following the horrific event at Burke's home, Vogel had initially suspected the theft of Perseus was a corporate espionage job by a rival tech firm or even an international cyber task force. Frankly, she had been so embroiled in worrying about Cal and then later returning to her duties at Langley that she had pushed the mystery aside.

Until Begley requested her to dig deep on Foley.

He must suspect, as I do, that Foley is tied up in all of this. But if he is, then who is sanctioning him? All clandestine activities and funding go directly through Begley.

She sighed, rubbing her neck. *Unless it's even higher up than any of our agencies.* Vogel thought of the implications. *Only one person besides Begley could create an off-the-books unit, but why would the President do that...unless he had doubts about his own immediate circle.*

As someone who controlled all seventeen of the intelligence agencies in the U.S., Begley wielded considerable power, which made her question why he would be resigning in less than a week.

Vogel removed a small flashlight from her desk drawer, activating the infra-red feature and directing it towards her bookcase, where she had previously identified a small hidden camera placed there by one of Begley's goons during their initial visit.

Vogel pulled her chair closer to the desk, typing furiously on her laptop. She pulled up an internal server, accessing an old account for a former member of her targeting team to avoid having any database searches immediately tracked back to her.

Vogel entered Begley's name and keywords related to shell corporations and privately owned businesses. She let her finger hover over the Enter button then bit her lower lip as she pressed down.

The data would be harvested from open source sites but also from NSA, FBI and CIA feeds along with any anomalies related to attempted elimination or scrubbing of such records, a unique capability specific only to Vogel's team of targeters.

Leaning back, she waited for the data to collate. A few minutes later, a listing of a half-dozen small businesses appeared. The odd assemblage of short-lived companies at different East Coast locations would strike the average person as a jumble of failed business attempts, but in Vogel's experience, the pattern reminded her of the numerous shell corporations that small terrorist cells relied on for distributing their funds, intel and weapons.

Upon closer scrutiny of one defunct company, she saw an entry related to a three-acre vacant lot that had been purchased eight years ago on the northwestern edge of Arlington and never developed.

She opened a new page, doing a records search for the site, but it only revealed that a smaller shell corporation had bought it for building a proposed public service company that never got off the ground.

Public service—that could mean a lot of things. Why the hell was Begley so interested in this spot?

Vogel pulled up another screen, studying the satellite images for that region of Arlington then zooming in on the tract of land. Her eyes widened at the sight of a small one-story facility at the location beside a single row of power-utility towers. A further search only revealed that the buildings were owned by Callen Incorporated. Vogel immediately switched back to the initial listing of businesses affiliated with Begley, seeing Callen listed at the bottom.

He's gone through a lot of trouble to keep the nature of that location a mystery. Something's not right, but it would take a team of analysts to sift through all of this, and I don't have that luxury.

Commotion in the hallway sliced through her concentration. Vogel felt her heart punching through her chest at the sound of someone barking at her staff. The familiar voice of the blonde-haired bodyguard who had accompanied Begley to her office a few days ago echoed off the walls, and she could hear her assistant trying to calm the man down.

Vogel copied the information on her screen to a flash-drive then connected it to her burner phone, sending the intel about the private utility company to Patterson, hoping he'd be able to figure out its significance. Once that was done, she pressed the numbers 219, which had been previously established as a distress signal with members of the SD unit in case they were ever abducted or in immediate danger.

Her office door slammed open, and the burly man stormed in, followed by two of Langley's armed security staff. Vogel recoiled into her seat at the violent entry.

She stood up, seeing the message had been sent then sliding the cellphone under the cushion of her seat.

Marcus, the armed security guard from the elevator entrance that she had greeted daily for four years, stepped up beside her, removing his handcuffs.

"You need to come with us, ma'am."

"For what?"

"We have orders that come directly from Director Jason Begley himself. Said you are to be arrested and detained for treason and the leaking of classified documents."

He leaned in as he was cuffing her. "Sorry, Ms. Vogel."

"Don't be sorry, fellas," said the bodyguard, raising his voice loud enough for the other staff in the tac-ops center to hear. "This traitorous bitch has been fooling you all, selling out our country. She has been in league with that fugitive Shepard, passing on classified documents over open channels while plotting against her superiors here. She'll be going away for a long, long time."

Once Vogel was cuffed, both guards held her arms at the elbows, escorting her out as the bodyguard unplugged her laptop and grabbed the files on her desk.

Vogel felt like a diver whose oxygen tank had just been ruptured, her chest constricting.

The confused and disillusioned eyes of her staff were fixated on her, burning through her as she was walked to the elevator.

She was escorted inside surrounded by all three men, who pressed in around her.

Her hands tightly bound before her.

Her vision narrowing.

And her legs trembling like the floor was about to give way into a black abyss.

FOLEY STEPPED AWAY from the planning room where his team was poring over electrical engineering schematics along the East Coast.

He removed the vibrating cellphone from his BDU pocket, noticing it was a number he'd not seen in some time.

And what Neil Patterson relayed to him during the next thirty seconds made the steely commander's heart race.

29

An hour into the drive from the tiger reserve, Shepard stopped the vehicle at a pull-off beside a river.

He rummaged through the Russians' belongings in the back seat, finding a backpack with an UZI and a half-dozen spare magazines, a medical kit, binoculars, condensed food packets and some water bottles.

Shepard did a chamber check on the UZI, placing it on the armrest, then slid the nearly depleted AK behind his seat. He handed Zemenova a water bottle, which she wasted little time in gulping down.

"You wanna tell me what you pulled off the dead guy in that cabin back there?"

She averted her eyes, opening the door then stepping out. "Nothing that concerns you."

"But clearly something that was worth risking getting shot for and probably the sole reason you made the trip out here."

He got out, moving around to the other side near a cluster of stumps centered around a campfire ring cluttered with trash.

"And don't tell me that guy was providing you with travel documents. He looked like a farmer, not someone who spent much time behind a keyboard. By the way you've handled yourself since we hit the trail yesterday, I'd say you've been to that park before."

"I never said I was getting travel documents. I said that I couldn't leave India until I got what I came for, and my friend Nihar back at the cabin was going to help me."

Zemenova's stomach still felt queasy from the constant adrenaline and stress coupled with a lack of food during the past twenty-four hours. She knew her only way out of this region and perhaps even the country was with the American. She still wasn't sure of the scope of his operation, but he would have access to resources or personnel for slipping across borders. Plus, she was sincere in her offer to help him with Burke's final request for Perseus.

But where is the rest of Stephen's research? Someone high up in the U.S. government must have it if they need me to reconfigure the source code. Her head was swirling with the strange turn of events since their arrival at the tiger preserve along with the heart-wrenching loss of her friend. Right now, she needed to continue fostering the American's trust and escape the reach of the Russian mob.

Zemenova sighed, feeling like she was back on the jungle trail, where one misstep could mean a deadly encounter with a predator.

She leaned back against the vehicle, removing the small nylon pouch from her cargo pants pocket. "When I relocated to India, Stephen placed me with a volunteer group in the preserve with a man he knew who had helped refugees and people fleeing from other countries for one reason or another. I lived with Nihar in the tiger preserve for the first four months, working with a few dozen other refugees, doing whatever manual labor was needed in exchange for room and board. Nihar was the director then and kept us tucked away at different jungle camps." She averted her eyes, staring at the ground. "He was one of the kindest people I've ever met. He dedicated his life to the service of others in a way that made me believe in humanity again... believe in living again."

She wiped a tear off her cheek, gazing up at the emerald canopy. "When Stephen finally secured a new identity for me, I left the community Nihar had fostered, and I relocated to Mumbai, leaving some of my belongings at the cabin back there."

She handed him the pouch. He shoved it back towards her. "Sorry, but I just don't trust you—you open it."

Zemenova frowned, pulling out a foot-long black cylinder that had two data entry ports on it.

"The hell is that thing?"

"Remember I told you that black box you have can hijack open communication sources? Well, this is the device that it's based on. Something I started before I fled Moscow. I was holding on to it in case the day ever came when I might need a bargaining chip with my old employers."

He rested his hand on his pistol as he walked back towards the driver's side. "Well, let's get a move on so we can make sure it doesn't come to that."

Victor pried open his crusty eyelids, the dried blood from a small gash on his forehead coating his face. From the smoldering remnants of nearby trees, he could tell that he'd been unconscious for a while after the vehicle explosion.

He forced himself up on one elbow, peering around at

the smoky terrain. To his right was one of his men with a hand-sized piece of metal shrapnel buried in his chest while hordes of black flies swarmed in and out of his gaping mouth.

Victor tottered up to a standing position, shaking his head.

"You okay, boss?" said his last remaining man to the left.

He answered with a grimace, picking up his Glock then trudging up the ash-covered slope towards the road, relieved to see that the local thugs had already cleared out, their remaining jeep still aflame amidst four charred corpses.

Victor walked in a large arc around the carnage, glancing up at the small shack and the shed. He peered around the back side, his stride quickening at the sight of a motorcycle with its key in the ignition.

He backed it out, checking the fuel gauge then starting the engine, yelling at his other man to move their dead compatriots' bodies from the road.

While he waited, Victor pulled out his iPhone, tapping a phone number on the cracked screen for his supplier in Mumbai.

"This is 719. I need additional assets—at least eight more men."

"Location?"

"I will contact you within two hours with that information. Just make sure they are equipped with Level II combat packages. There's going to be a small war unfolding soon. And get me satellite footage from my present coordinates. I need to track a man and a woman in a Land Rover who just fled this region."

30

THE ROUTE to New Delhi was only eighty-three miles, but it took nearly three hours due to the poorly maintained roads and the constant traffic snarls as they approached the outskirts.

Between the pedestrians, the endless goats and pigs in the streets, and the chaotic mix of cars, flatbed delivery trucks, scooters, bicycles and sea of three-wheeled auto rickshaws, Cal realized how much he appreciated the organized congestion of New York City traffic.

The jungle and farms had disappeared a half-hour earlier, and the primeval aroma of the forest was replaced with an amalgam of odors from vehicle emissions, perspiration and open food markets in the stifling humidity of the midday sun.

They headed south through the modernized mass of neighborhoods in the capital city of New Delhi, whose architecture was meant to symbolize British supremacy in the region during that nation's occupation, unlike the southern half of the city known as Delhi, which retained the indigenous influences of its Hindu-Islamic roots, which stretched back to the city's origins centuries earlier.

It was on the cusp between the modern and the traditional worlds that Cal was headed, and he drove for another thirty minutes to a ramshackle neighborhood peppered with weathered apartment buildings, street vendors and tin-roofed shacks along the Yamuna River that skirted the east side of downtown.

After exiting the highway, Cal turned left down a two-lane blacktop road whose spider web cracks were clogged with trampled weeds. He pulled into a dirt parking lot near a cluster of townhomes overlooking the train tracks.

Zemenova craned her head, staring out at the bustling suburbs in the distance. "This is where your safehouse is?"

"Hardly. But this pricey vehicle will fit in here better than in the neighborhood where we're heading, and we won't be using it again." He slid the UZI into his pack then leaned in back, quickly disassembling the bolt from the AK to render it inoperable since the weapon was too lengthy to bring along.

"We've got two miles on foot to cover, so stay close to me. We have to assume those gang members back at the park have eyes on these streets."

THE WALK through the city was uneventful, and they melted into the bustling crowds filling the sidewalks, which seemed to be crammed with every food and spice vendor from the continent, eventually peeling off near an older section of apartments with flaking paint and whose porches were lined with clothes hung out to dry.

Cal walked past a dilapidated playground whose broken

metal slides looked like they were a surefire recipe for a tetanus shot.

He descended a flight of stairs on the shaded east side of the four-story building then swung open a mesh gate that led down a hundred-foot-long cement corridor with slats in the right edge of the ceiling for letting in sunlight.

Stepping over the squashed remains of a large centipede being feasted upon by ants, he and Zemenova continued down the corridor, arriving at a utility room door at the end.

"I hope that's not a broom closet," she quipped.

"A little roomier than that." He gave a series of knocks on the door, but he knew the micro-cameras he'd earlier embedded along the hallway had already revealed his presence to the occupants inside.

"This used to be an old British safehouse back in the day. The walls and ceiling are a couple feet of concrete with a reinforced steel entrance."

The door unlocked, swinging open. He wasn't expecting the sudden rush of Viper's arms around him as she gave him a hearty hug. "God, what took you so long? When you texted that you were walking here on foot, I didn't think it would take two hours."

He stepped inside, nodding at Aden and Sayyid in the other room. "I had a little run-in with some surprise visitors at the park, so we needed to make sure we took a long walk around the city before showing up here."

Cal motioned for the woman to come inside, giving her a hasty introduction to the others.

"So, you're the one?" said Viper, scrutinizing the tired woman's face and the lacerations on her arms. "Been on a jungle adventure, it looks like." She motioned for the woman to follow her to the back bedroom, handing her a towel and pointing to some clothes hanging in the closet.

"Thanks," Zemenova said, immediately heading into the bathroom and closing the door.

Viper walked to the kitchen, sidling up next to Cal, who was wolfing down a banana. "Well, what did you learn? Something promising, I hope."

Cal leaned against the counter, licking his lips and fighting back a crooked grin. "Maybe you should pull up a chair."

31

THE OUTSKIRTS **of Western Delhi**

UPON HEARING a cluster of vehicles pulling into the driveway behind his country estate, Rohan Patel, the patriarch of the Naja Crime Syndicate, crushed out his cigarette on the marble windowsill. He stood up, sauntering to the back porch, where a handful of his men were carefully extricating his son Sai from the rear of a Mercedes van. The pale-faced man lay limp as he was carried on a blanket-turned-stretcher into the shade of a large almond tree near the porch.

"He took an AK round to the stomach, boss," said the bare-chested driver as he nervously moved up alongside Rohan.

"From who? You guys were supposed to do the fucking shooting."

"The American...same guy who..."

Patel thrust his meaty hand around the guy's throat,

shoving him up against the tree trunk. "The one who killed Adesh? You mean that fuckin' guy?"

The gasping man squeaked out a wispy response. "We were surprised by...by some other hitters who showed up... sounded like they were Russian."

"Russians? You sure? They mostly stick to the coastal cities." Rohan released his grip, pushing the man into a small table that upended from his weight. Rohan paced around the patio. "So, the Ivans must have hired a freelancer to do their bidding."

The older man brushed the others aside, staring down at his eldest son, whose clammy face had already attracted a cluster of flies. He traced his eyes down to the oozing wound leaking through layers of rags on his abdomen then tapped his sandaled foot against Sai's leg. "You're gonna get through this, boy. I've been shot worse than that—twice, actually— and I'm still here."

He grabbed the nearest henchman by the arm. "Take him inside and get him some water, keep him cool then get that old British doctor from the infirmary. Tell him it's the usual patch-up job and not to waste any time in getting here."

The man dutifully nodded, trotting down the driveway towards a motorcycle.

Rohan leaned over, seizing Sai's pale chin as the man groaned. "I need you back on your feet by next week to handle that opium shipment coming in from Bangladesh, so get your shit together, boy."

He grabbed Sai's second-in-command as the burly man walked by. "Get the word out on the street—I want every drug dealer, thief and user looking for this American, from here to Mumbai. Circulate his photo around and tell 'em there's 2 million rupees on his head, then let our old associates with the Russian mob down south know that we put a bounty out on their guy and see how they react."

"You got it, boss."

Rohan rested his right hand on the ebony-handled 1911 pistol on his hip. "Fucking Russians think they can move in on my turf, they'll have a war they won't believe."

32

VIPER HAD COOKED up a curry chicken noodle dish with onions and pigeon peas while Cal got Zemenova set up on the laptop in the living room then let her get to work.

She attached the ether cords to the black box then to the ruggedized laptop. A password prompt showed up, causing her to glance up at Cal.

"What? I figured you would know."

"And if you hadn't located me, how would you have accessed this?"

"I probably would have been forced to abduct someone versed in hacking." He flung his hands up in the air. "But, hell, I did find you, and here we are."

She bit her lower lip, her eyes darting along the floor, then she typed in a series of alphanumeric figures that opened a portal on the screen, revealing several sequences of code that were indecipherable to Cal.

Zemenova looked up at him then the others at the opposite end of the room. "This will take me a few hours by the looks of it. I need to first analyze what Stephen overlaid onto my original source work, then I will have to configure it so it can be transferred."

"But not on that laptop, right?" said Cal. "My understanding is that the system is not equipped for something on that scale."

"You are correct. I can examine the files and do the necessary adjustments on the code to prime it for acceptance into the mainframes with your counterparts, but this can only be transferred to your colleagues using the type of hardware found at a cyber firm."

"That's what I figured," Cal sighed, tossing his baseball cap on the table and running his hands through his hair.

"Why don't you keep going while Cal and I discuss some of our options," Viper said to the woman. She tugged on Cal's shirt sleeve, motioning for him to follow her into the other room while Zemenova hunched over the makeshift workspace.

Viper checked to make sure they were out of earshot from the woman as she leaned in closer to Cal. "Look, I know you're spent and just want this to be over. So do I, but you've been runnin' point on this op for too long. It's time to reach out and get some help."

Cal sighed, folding his arms. "You don't think I'm prepared to go the distance, is that it?"

She rested her hand on his shoulder. "You've already gone the distance several times over in the past two months and, frankly, I'm not even sure how you're still standing. This isn't a question of your commitment, dammit. I've known you long enough to see when you're running on empty, and now isn't the time to go it alone...not when we're so close to completing what you set out to do."

She removed a burner phone from her pocket, pressing it into Cal's hand. "Make the call. It's time." Viper took a step back, leaning in the doorway. "You always told me that the forethought that goes into executing a mission should be carried through right to the last second until your boots are on the ground back home. That the end game is as critical as the launch plan."

Cal looked down at the phone, rubbing his finger along the sides as if it retained mystical properties. He knew Viper was right, as usual. She always possessed such clarity and logic at the times when he was lacking those qualities from sheer exhaustion or faced with the inner turmoil that had embodied his life for the past few months.

Just stay the course a little longer, then you're done with all of it.

He craved the freedom of relinquishing, even if forcibly, the hold that the recent past and this commitment to Burke held over him. He had to finish this before it pulled him so far under there would be no means of finding a sliver of light at the surface.

Stay the course. You can do this. You have to.

He closed the door, flipping open the phone and pressing the lone number programmed into the device.

VIPER GRABBED her tawny-colored pack off the floor then pulled up a battered chair, sitting down beside the woman. Viper unzipped the main compartment, pulling out a large hard-drive and tapping her fingers on it.

"When you're done with that, I need you to do one more thing," Viper said.

Zemenova's focused expression changed to one of concern. "Where did you get that?"

"It was liberated from a shipment in Bulgaria."

"I haven't seen one like this in quite a while." The woman gently handled the shiny black box, turning it over like she was an antiquities inspector. "These are only used by the military for weaponized malware."

Viper grinned. "Yep."

33

ARLINGTON, **Virginia**

JASON BEGLEY LET the leggy blonde woman in the black skirt exit the elevator first, stealing another glance at her as he stepped out and headed through the parking structure of the NSA building towards his Audi.

A minute later, he caught sight of a familiar figure to the right, his stomach tightening at the etched face of Ryan Foley, who was walking towards him.

"Jason, it's been a while. How's life in the trenches of D.C.?"

"Ryan, well, uhm, this is the last place I ever expected to see you." Begley adjusted his laptop bag on his shoulder, extending an anemic handshake out to the man.

"Yeah, my business takes me all over these days."

"And what business is that, exactly, since you're no longer heading up the SD units?"

"Oh, I've got my blades in different forges at the moment." He glanced at a red Jaguar exiting the parking garage. "How about you? Heard you were stepping down from your position. You moving into the private sector or just taking a breather from federal work for a while?"

"Breather for sure. Taking the wife and stepdaughter to Florida then sailing down to the Caribbean for a few weeks. Who knows after that?"

He glanced over Foley's muscular arms, seeing the surly operator was still keeping active for a guy his age but noticing that he lacked his usual dark tan from spending so much time in the field.

What the hell is he doing here?

"Well, good, you've certainly had enough time on the political frontlines to warrant a break." Foley pointed his finger at him. "As I recall, you started working on the Hill as an aide to the CIA director twenty or so years ago after law school, right?"

Begley nodded. "Good memory. Twenty-three years ago actually, and yes, I served under Director Tanner for a few years before moving into a leadership role at the NSA."

What's he fishing for? That's ancient history.

Foley nodded. "There was another guy I remember...a little older... Uhm...shit, I can't recall his name, but he was a southerner with a thick accent, and that back-slapping charm 'n all. He also worked on a senate subcommittee briefly with Tanner then, same time as you. Nicest guy in the world. I had only been with the agency a few years after my SF days...damned if I can remember who that was though."

Begley felt an icy chill run down his back, knowing he was hinting at Edgeworth, who had worked with Director Tanner on increasing funding to the agency's satellite surveillance division. It was how Begley and the now-senator had met.

"Afraid my memory is spotty on those old days," said Begley with a plastic smile.

"Old days are right, for both of us. That was when a person could have some relative measure of trust in the guy up the food chain within clandestine services to adhere to a code of conduct, personally and professionally. Even that is becoming a distant memory." He took a step closer, his voice lowering. "You know, we always had this saying in special-ops: *The mission, the men then me.* These days, for a lot of people working up on the Hill who are 5,000 miles from the battlefield, it's more like: *Me and my own personal mission.*"

Begley frowned, thumbing towards the exit to the street. "Except now, the battlefield is only a few hundred yards away on our own soil, Ryan, and the game is a little different than it was twenty years ago. That's something a lot of people not in the trenches of D.C. on a daily basis have little understanding of or want to even admit to."

Foley's gaze felt like it was stabbing straight through to the back of Begley's skull. The swarthy operator's grim expression changed to a wolfish smile. "Well, then it's good that people like us who know both sides can talk in person about the realities of life...and death, neither of which ever play out much like a *game*, in my experience."

Yeah, sure. Shouldn't you return to the fossil display case at the fucking museum already?

Begley was relieved when Foley looked down at his watch then extended his hand. "I better get a run on it, Jason. Take care and enjoy that time off with your family."

He tried to respond with a firm grip but was met with nearly crushing force from Foley's handshake.

"See you around, Ryan."

Or not, you crusty motherfucker.

Begley got into his car, certain that Foley was aware of his connection to Senator Edgeworth.

But what else does he know?

Begley felt his heart racing, swiveling in his seat to search the parking structure for Foley, but the man was already gone. He thought back over their physical distance and contact, which only consisted of a single handshake. He glanced over his wrist and jacket sleeve, certain that the man couldn't have placed a bug.

How could he? It was just a handshake. He's not a fucking ninja. At least that's what Begley repeatedly tried to convince himself of on his drive home.

AFTER HIS BRIEF encounter with Begley, Foley walked a circuitous route through the city for four blocks. He paused at a side street across from a white Sprinter van adorned with the logo for a bug extermination company.

He glanced back at the alley then at the pedestrians on the sidewalks to the right before heading towards the van. Climbing in through the back doors, he moved up behind Kyle West, who was seated at an elongated desk, monitoring the visual feeds of the parking garage where Begley had been situated a few minutes earlier.

West pivoted on his round stool. "He made a call on a burner phone as soon you two finished talking."

"To who?" said Foley, removing his jacket.

"Unknown, but I pinpointed the location of the number —it's currently mobile." He enhanced the map image on his laptop, showing a red blip moving west along a secondary highway near the West Virginia border. "Not much out there except some small towns and plenty of mountains."

Foley's face grew taut. After getting a call from Neil Patterson about Vogel being forcibly removed from Langley two hours ago, he knew the sand in her hourglass was diminishing with each passing minute.

"Good place for a black site...or to dump a body."

He moved past the surveillance equipment, sliding into the driver's seat just as the passenger's door opened. Erica Hamill, the blonde woman from the elevator in the parking structure, entered.

"The audio device is in place on Begley's laptop case," she said, stepping into the rear and slipping out of her skirt and heels then donning a black jumpsuit and boots.

Foley fired up the engine, glancing back at West.

"We don't have much time, so ready the assault gear while I get us to our helo at the airfield."

"Should I alert Nolan and the rest of our personnel to join us?" said Hamill.

"Negative. Nolan's halfway across the ocean by now, inbound to Shepard's location," said Foley. "And this is going to be a hasty extraction, so it'll just have to be us."

And pray that we make it to you in time, Lynn.

34

VOGEL FELT the bumpy transition in the road, figuring the van had just left a highway and was bobbing along a rutted dirt road.

She figured they had been driving for nearly an hour, and the lack of other vehicular noises meant they were either in the less-populated areas to the southwest of Arlington or somewhere near West Virginia. Either one indicated they were far from people, and she fought the stomach-churning image of being taken to some secluded cabin to be tied up and tortured for days.

Vogel could barely lean forward, her ankles shackled to U-bolts welded to the floor. The view through the front window was partly obscured by the steel mesh separating the prisoner containment area from the driver's compartment.

"Where the hell are you taking me? The agency holding facility is back near Arlington."

Begley's bristle-headed henchman who had stormed into her office swiveled towards her. "We got a nice place in the woods for you, sweetie, don't worry."

"Is that what you do for Begley? You're just his lapdog who dry-humps his leg whenever he looks at you, then goes off to handle his dirty work?"

"Shut up, bitch, or I'll wrap those chains around your throat." He turned around as the driver took a sharp turn, the lanky man muttering a curse as the van came to a halt thirty feet from a large fallen tree across the dirt road.

"Just go around it," said the bodyguard. "There's some flat ground to the..."

A barrage of gunfire erupted, and the front windshield was peppered with multiple rounds that fractured the glass.

Vogel secreted herself against the wall, her breathing constricting as the cacophony of machinegun fire continued, wondering if the van was going topple over from the deafening impact.

ONCE WEST AND Hamill had disabled the engine and front tires with 10mm rounds from their MP5s, Foley moved onto the road, squaring off with the front of the van and firing two shots of Quadrangle Buckshot from his Mossberg 500 into the center of the armored glass until a small gap was evident. The third shot consisted of a CS grenade whose soft nose ruptured upon impacting the jagged hole, delivering tear gas inside the van. The initial assault unfolded smoothly, as it had for him during countless abductions in hostile countries.

The three operators moved in unison, with West and Hamill blasting open the door locks on either side then yanking out the gagging thugs while Foley breached the rear hatch. He slid on his gas mask, hopping inside and removing the bolt-cutters from his pack then severing Vogel's leg shackles.

He grabbed her arm, yelling at her to follow him as he guided her towards the opening. Foley jumped down, scooping her up off her feet and carrying her to the edge of the forest.

VOGEL FELT like her head had been dunked in acid, her throat and eyes burning as she fought to breathe. The mysterious figure in black who snatched her from the van was clearly a pro, but right now all she could think about was catching her breath then running like hell, if her lungs would allow it.

She sputtered out another labored cough then gulped in a breath of cool air, lying back as her eyes continued tearing up.

"Clear," shouted a man's voice to the front of the vehicle, followed by the same response issued by a woman.

Vogel sat up, rubbing her bleary eyes, then saw the man in front of her remove his gas mask and press the mask to her face. She breathed in the welcome rush of oxygen, her right hand slowly reaching around her side and settling upon a fist-sized rock.

With her head and vision clearing, she clutched the weapon, tracing her eyes up the man's stocky frame towards his creased face.

Colonel Foley.

She wasn't sure if she muttered it aloud, but she flung off the mask, releasing the rock and staggering to her feet.

She wanted to throw her arms around him, a nervous smile creaking out from her red cheeks. He moved closer, resting his hand on her shoulder and pulling her in for a hug.

"Lynn...am I ever glad to see you."

———

FOLEY LET OUT a sigh of relief, motioning for Vogel to sit back down, but she refused. Her smile quickly faded as she glared at the two captives being escorted towards the back of the van by Hamill and Nolan.

Vogel handed the gas mask back to Foley then stalked forward, sending a vicious shin kick into the bodyguard's groin then smashing her elbow into his jaw. The man collapsed onto the road, his cheek reddening as he groaned.

"That's for threatening to hurt my sister, you bastard."

The two operators stepped back, looking at the fiery woman then over at Foley, who lightly shrugged his shoulders.

The colonel moved closer to her as she was raising her leg for a kick to the man's head. "I know about what happened, Lynn. Patterson filled me in. I promise that these guys, and Begley himself, will answer for what they've done, but right now, I need their jaws intact."

She blew a strand of hair off her nose, reluctantly stepping back. Foley knelt down beside the moaning figure, grabbing his neck. "Where were you heading? Does Begley have a safehouse out here?"

The man coughed then spit onto Foley's vest. The colonel dropped the goon's head then stood up, moving to the driver, who was thrashing at his Flex-cuff restraints as he tried to pull away from Hamill. She slammed her boot into the back of his left leg, driving him onto his knees.

"Look, man, I was just hired to get her from Point A to Point B. I don't know anything about the rest of the op."

Foley stood a foot from the man. "Funny, but I know a helluva lot of guys in clandestine ops, and you don't look like one of 'em. Begley farm you out of a private contracting firm, or are you a recruit from a new unit of his own design?"

The man shifted his nervous gaze between the operators then glanced back at Foley. "I don't know anyone named Begley. I told you, I was just paid to drive."

Foley shook his head, removing his folding knife and flicking it open. He grabbed the man's flossy black hair, pulling his head to the side then resting the blade tip on the man's right cheek. "I don't have time for twenty questions, so you have five seconds to reconsider."

"Fuck you, old man."

A downward flick of Foley's wrist delivered a C-shaped slice that cut deeply into the flesh. The man howled, backpedaling before being restrained by Hamill as a rivulet of blood dripped off his chin.

Foley slid closer, pointing the blade at the man's left eye. "My patience grows thin, so this will be the last time. Where were you heading?"

"You talk and I'll kill you myself," shouted the body-guard who was being restrained by Nolan.

Foley slid his blade closer to the driver's eye. "There is a fate worse than death, trust me."

"Alright, stop, goddammit. We were taking her to an abandoned farmhouse about ten miles from here. Begley wanted us to hold her there in case she was needed."

"Needed for what?" said Vogel, stepping up next to Foley.

The man brushed his shoulder up against his bleeding

cheek. "For leverage...against Shepard. He planned to film you being tortured then executed if Shepard didn't comply with his demands to turn over whatever the hell Begley's after."

She narrowed her eyes, pressing her hands against her stomach. "You're not agency, you're a fucking animal."

Foley lowered his blade, folding it and sliding it back into his pocket. "Just one more thing. Begley's main entrance into his black site in Arlington, at the top of the medical building—what is in there, and how many personnel are present?"

"Never been. I was strictly transport."

Foley studied the man's face for a long moment then deftly removed the suppressed Glock 19 from his holster and fired a single round into the driver's forehead. He collapsed back, rolling off the dirt shoulder into the ditch below.

The colonel turned around and pointed his weapon at the bodyguard, who was shaking his head.

"Wait, wait, I can still be of value. I know a shit-ton about Begley's operations."

"Not likely, or he wouldn't have risked sending you out here. Besides, you threatened someone very dear to me." He squeezed off two rounds into the man's skull, blowing out the back of his head.

Vogel's hands shook as if she had fired the shots. She felt no remorse over what had just unfolded but an odd blend of terror mixed with relief. She had only witnessed Foley eliminating hostiles in foreign countries via long-range satellite and drone images. All of those were sanctioned strikes carried out on well-known terrorist targets or factions.

Now, he had just been judge and executioner on American soil.

Is he running his own show with no one to answer to, or is he working for someone so high up in the government that he has free rein to do whatever is needed to keep the country safe?

Her head was swimming with questions, but right now she just wanted to get as far from this forest as possible and call her sister. Beyond that, she had no idea what was going to come of her life and career, which were two nearly indistinguishable realities and all she'd ever known.

35

Delhi

"THEY ENTERED the lower level of that apartment complex," said Bishop in his earpiece to his three other operators spread around the alleys below as he scanned the buildings in either direction from his rooftop perch across the street.

The burly henchman kneeling beside him pointed to the satellite and thermal images on his tablet. "I can pick up the other residents in that building even in the basement, but there's one apartment in the northeast corner that is not registering...not a thing. That has to be where they're located. It must have some blackout material or a device shielding that area."

"What about egress routes to and from that place?" said Bishop. "They have to have at least one other way out of there that we're not seeing."

"We're assuming it's just Shepard and the woman in there, but he could have a handful of PMCs or former assets with him too," said the bearded man to Bishop's right, who was scanning the apartment windows through the scope on his suppressed AR-10.

"Safe to assume he's got some old contacts in this country, even though Begley said the guy has been cut off and running solo since he fled the U.S."

He leaned over, grabbing the tablet out of his henchman's hands and scrutinizing the image. "We can't risk waiting. We need to see what's going down in there. If he's got the place blacked out, then he may be trying to upload the source code to someone."

He tapped on his ear-mic. "Bravo Three, take up a position at the other emergency exit in the apartment. Bravo One and Two, head down into the stairwell and proceed towards the northeast apartment. We'll be right behind you, then we'll breach the door and proceed inside."

He patted the bearded man on the shoulder. "Stay here and provide overwatch. Any squirters make it outside this building then drop 'em."

36

SINCE THEY HAD ARRIVED at the safehouse, Theresa Zemenova had hardly moved from her seat, working rapid-fire on the laptop to configure Burke's source code so it would be compatible with the Perseus mainframes.

Where the latter was located was still unknown to her, but she suspected it wasn't with the CIA, given Shepard's ragtag group and the little she had gleaned from the man about his weary trek around India to locate her.

Is he out on a limb with his handlers back in the States, using the source code as a bargaining tool to regain his status with the CIA, or are he and his friends running a lone-wolf operation for someone outside of the government?

By the man's haggard appearance, she wasn't sure that any of those things really mattered to him. The hollowness in his eyes reminded her of soldiers back home who were coping with the ravaging effects of severe PTSD. She couldn't tell if his exceedingly violent reactions in recent battles with the Russian and Indian gangs were reflexive or if he was someone whose life was only fueled by brutality, alternating between being the hunter and the hunted.

Maybe that's all there is for someone like him, but what kind of life is that.

"What's your timeline?" Shepard said, coming up behind her and handing her another cup of chai tea laced with coffee.

"I'm finishing up right now actually, then I just have to review a few things." She patted her hand on the stolen military hard-drive that Viper had acquired in Bulgaria. "And I already completed the modifications you requested for this device."

"Good. When you're done, take a break for a while, then we'll be heading southwest towards a small airfield not far from here...that is, if you're still up for our company."

She straightened up, glancing up at him briefly. "Of course. Besides, I'd rather not be wandering around India on my own right now."

He patted her on the shoulder. "I know we only met yesterday and you've already been through the wringer with all that's happened, but thanks for sticking it out with me."

Zemenova nodded. "Anything for Stephen Burke...and his friends."

She heard him walk away, finishing her work on the laptop then pulling up a screen she'd minimized earlier when he approached. Zemenova leaned in closer, examining an image of a tall building on the west end of Moscow, the outline of a familiar cyber facility—and one of the main reasons that she had agreed to help Shepard—drawing her attention.

CAL WALKED into the small kitchen area, standing across from Aden and Sayyid, who were downing another plateful of chicken and noodles.

Aden slid over a foot, motioning towards Shepard to partake of the serving bowl on the counter.

"No, thanks." He grinned, moving in closer and whispering, "I try to avoid the meals that Samira makes. Not enough Tums in this city."

"I heard that, Cal," she said from her seat in the other room, leaning her head and sneering at him. "At least I *can* cook instead of that ketchup-laced slop you make."

"You never used to complain when we were deployed on long ops overseas."

"Maybe you're not the listener you think you are. I always complained...it was just in the form of me drowning out your meals with Tabasco."

"Which is basically ketchup with hot sauce, you know."

The two Syrian men laughed, nearly choking on their food. "You two bicker like a brother and sister," said Sayyid.

"Except if she was my sister, my old man would have kicked her out to the barn when she was a kid with her attitude."

Her stern voice emanated from the other room. "That'll cost you a rib the next time we practice our combatives drills."

"Yeah, yeah." Cal shook his head, chuckling. He piled a heaping spoonful of the vegetable and chicken dish onto his plate.

The forkful of food almost made it to his lips when Viper's laptop began blaring. Instantly, Cal's stomach coiled up, knowing their external security alarms had just been tripped. He flung his plate on the table, rushing out of the kitchen, his concealed Glock already free of its holster.

Viper was hunched over her laptop as the others gathered around her, studying the four camera angles in the outlying hallways and stairwells, where five heavily armed men were cautiously making their way towards the safehouse. By their accoutrements and the fluidity of their movements, he could tell they weren't the Russian goons from earlier.

"That looks like an agency snatch-and-grab team," said Viper.

"Not sure, but we need to get the hell out of here. Go; I'll hold them off," Cal shouted.

The two Syrian men hastily gathered their packs and weapons, heading to the rear bedroom, flipping over a cot in the corner and lifting up a heavy rug concealing a steel floor hatch.

Zemenova shut down the laptop, handing the black box and the weaponized malware device to Viper, who stowed them in her shoulder bag.

Cal retrieved an MK12 and a Remington 870 shotgun from the corner, pausing next to Viper for a moment, both of them exchanging knowing looks.

"I thought we'd have more time, dammit," he yelled.

"I know."

He watched her descend then handed down the two remaining MP7 rifles.

Cal got into position beside the reinforced concrete half-wall twenty feet from the main entrance, the Remington pointed at the door. He glanced at the video footage again, seeing the lead man in the strike team placing a licorice-like segment of plastic explosives along the hinged portion of the steel door to the safehouse.

Cal retreated from the living room into the back

bedroom, lowering his MK12 into the four-foot-high tunnel then climbing down.

He stood on the dirt floor, his head protruding from the opening, taking one last glance at the video images that showed the mercs stacking up in the hallway as the lead man prepared to breach the front door.

Cal quickly retrieved a frag grenade from his backpack then closed the hatch, leaving it unlocked.

Fifteen seconds. He knew exactly what was about to unfold from years of being on the other end.

Explosive entry.

Flash-bangs.

Assault.

Kill or capture.

Gather intel.

Then stow-and-go or *stay-and-play*.

He hoped the latter lingo for enhanced interrogation was outside of the day's events.

A part of him just wanted to hold his ground and engage his pursuers, destroying them or being destroyed.

Either or both would be OK with me.

But there were other people to think about. He'd gotten Samira and her friends into this, and he had to see this mission through to the end before his own fate could be in his control again, if the latter was even possible.

His mind shot back to the present as the explosion rattled the six-inch-thick steel hatch. He felt the percussive blasts from three flash-bangs then waited a second before flinging open the hatch, tossing the live grenade into the room and dropping the lid shut again and rotating the locking bolts into place.

He squatted in the narrow tunnel, grabbing his rifle then

trotting down the passage as the walls behind him rumbled and dirt shook loose from above.

He knew any survivors would quickly muster their remaining numbers and breach the hatch, but life now was all about buying time for his small team and getting the source code uploaded.

Weeks of uncertainty to get to this moment, and now everything hinges on what happens in the next few hours.

VIPER PLODDED through the ankle-deep sewer water in the tunnel as they crouch-trotted to the first junction, sixty feet from the hatch they'd descended.

She tried to convince herself that the distant noises near the safehouse were from the clanking of steam-pressured pipes and not from multiple explosions, but she knew all too well the familiar sound associated with breaching and its aftermath.

She paused, looking back down the tunnel for signs of Shepard.

"Goddammit, Cal. What are you up to now?"

She hoped there was some tactical motive he had for lingering behind longer than he should have, trying to drive away the thought that he was, consciously or not, seeking his own end.

No, that can't be why you stayed. But even she wasn't sure anymore. *And that hatch would have held them off long enough for all of us to escape, so what the fuck were you thinking, staying to engage them?*

She shined her UV flashlight down the passage to the right, picking up the marks they'd previously painted on the tunnel then pushing into a larger tunnel for a hundred yards before veering to the left.

Sunlight was streaming in through the rusty grate at the end. Viper clutched the critical components in her shoulder bag, her heart racing as much from their harried movement as from her sinking concern over Cal's fate. She forced herself forward, picking up her pace as the others followed in earnest.

A few minutes later, her fears were allayed when Cal emerged from the tunnel.

He looked over everyone then moved up next to Zemenova. "You alright?"

"Is this a regular thing for you, getting into shootouts every couple of hours?" she said.

"Sure seems like it lately."

"Yeah, it's a thing," quipped Viper.

"Where to now?" the woman said.

"We're going to head towards an airstrip by the town of Kablana, thirty kilometers southwest of here. That's our next stop...and hopefully our last."

He thrust his chin at the tree-lined stream ahead that led to a small bridge. "But first, we need some new wheels."

BISHOP CREPT out from behind the shrapnel-riddled table that he'd flipped upon seeing the grenade hurtling towards them from the back room. Other than a few lacerations on his neck from flying splinters, he was unscathed, but he couldn't say the same for Arlen, the black operator splayed on the floor in the corner with an arterial pool of blood beside his shredded thighs.

Bishop coughed, gagging from all the drywall dust in the

air then stood up, scanning his remaining four men. He motioned to the living quarters to the right. "See if there's any salvageable intel, then we'll retrace our steps back out of here and see if we can pick up their trail in the city."

"Why not use the tunnel and head after 'em?" said the lanky mercenary by the door.

"This part of the city is so old, there's probably dozens of catacombs below us, and I'm sure Shepard has his egress route already rigged with a shitload of booby-traps." He stepped out into the hallway, rubbing his eyes, then changed the frequency on his ear-mic, contacting Dennis Palermo back in Virginia.

"They were ready for us and escaped through some tunnels."

"What do you need from me?" said Palermo.

"They're going to stay on the run. The train and local transport are going to be too risky now, especially since they've pissed off the main crime syndicate here from the local chatter I picked up, and they probably have more Russkies on their tail."

He paced back and forth in the hallway, hearing the drone of police sirens in the distance who were probably enroute to the blown-out apartment. "If I were Shepard, I'd be looking for a low-profile way out of India. He's probably got that contingency already handled."

He could hear Palermo typing. "The Delhi International Airport is on the other side of the city."

"Nah, too many cameras and cops there. Do you get what *low profile* fucking means?"

"The only other options are the bus station at the south end, or there's a small airstrip about thirty minutes south-west of your location."

Bishop balled his fist. "Get me what you can on the

airstrip and send me the coordinates, then scan every street cam and surveillance image on this side of the city to pinpoint Shepard." He watched his men exit the apartment, plucking wood debris from their vests and clothing. "Shouldn't be too hard to find—he leaves a shitload of destruction in his wake."

37

WEST BALTIMORE

AFTER A FORTY-MINUTE FLIGHT in the dark, the last fifteen minutes of which involved being blindfolded, Vogel felt the helicopter set down.

Once the rotors came to a standstill, she was helped from the cabin by West and led by her arm along a gritty asphalt surface into an elevator, where they descended for what felt like four floors.

Foley was to her right and had informed her that these security measures were temporary and that she would soon be at his new base of operations.

But base for what? This can't be anything official.

The elevator doors slid open, and Foley removed her blindfold.

"Please come with me, Lynn. We don't have a lot of time."

There was an industrial odor in the air, a blend of new construction amidst a musty aroma.

She followed behind him as the other members of his team peeled off to either side, heading to either a gear repository on the right or towards the comms center on the left, which was little more than several rows of collapsible tables filled with electronics hardware and laptops.

"We've only been here about a month and are still working out the kinks on our setup, so you'll have to pardon the dust," said Foley.

He seemed so businesslike, a far cry from the pistol-wielding executioner she'd witnessed in action an hour ago.

Foley removed his tac-vest, dropping it on a desk, then continued towards the center of the warehouse, where a half-dozen men and women were busy working at a large table comprised of several plywood sheets suspended on rusty barrels.

Surrounding the table full of maps and photos were six upright whiteboards, each divided into counties in Virginia and Maryland, while the others contained information related to Mumbai, New Delhi, Kolkata and other regions in India.

Peppered throughout many of the diagrams was Shepard's name along with dates and GPS coordinates, though she couldn't tell if he was a part of Foley's operation or someone on their pursuit list.

All roads lead back to Cal. What the hell has he gotten into... or never gotten out of to begin with?

Vogel's head was on a swivel, examining the rows of mainframe computers to her right, which occupied a fifty-by-fifty-foot section of the warehouse basement. Beyond that was a vault-like structure whose open door revealed an armory equipped with weapons and tactical gear similar to the one at Langley.

To her left were a dozen desks spread out in a half-circle

with a dual-faced monitor in the middle, showing real-time satellite footage of Southeast Asia. The analysts were all unfamiliar faces working on ruggedized laptops the likes of which she hadn't seen before.

Vogel felt like she had entered a nether region within clandestine services whose budget exceeded that of even her division of targeters.

"This is impressive, Colonel."

"It's still in its infancy, but it'll do for now. This site is only for housing the Perseus mainframes and some of my team. Otherwise, we are intended to be a fully mobile operation, able to pick up and relocate to wherever we're needed, via plane, ship or direct insertion."

Her mouth hung open. "So, you are the one who stole Perseus from Burke's company?"

"I wish I could make that boast, but it was your old boss, Patterson, actually, who was the man behind the curtain. He didn't want, rather couldn't risk, having it fall into Begley's hands after what happened to Burke, and he already had plans and a team in place in the event something catastrophic ever occurred."

Vogel grit her teeth, grateful that the tech wasn't in Begley's possession but wanting to lash out in rage whenever she heard the man's name.

"And your new crew here does what, exactly?"

"I've named it the Critical Response Team or CRT, and we go wherever we're needed within our own borders or abroad."

She gave him a suspicious look. "Since you're at the helm, I assume the *need* refers to threat elimination and not intel gathering?"

"Despite what you witnessed earlier, it's both actually, but I'll have to get back with you in six months on which side the scales will tip, as we are just getting up and running."

"Where is your funding coming from? Not the agency, or Begley wouldn't have needed me to track you down."

Foley crossed his arms. "My unit answers only to the President, and our mission is determined by the threat our nation is facing that day, week or month. Our focus here is a little different than what you were doing with the SD units. Those missions were conducted internationally and presented a clear target to strike." He waved his hand out towards the desks of analysts. "Right now, all you need to know is that our singular objective is in providing support to Cal."

She canted her head. "What is he in possession of that Begley, and you, would direct all of your resources to finding him? I thought Cal went dark, for good, until Begley showed up in my office and threatened to tear apart my world unless I helped him."

Foley motioned with his hand to a man with a trim beard seated at the main computer terminals to the right. "When we arrived at this site over a month ago and began putting Perseus to task, my cyber expert, Kyle West, whom you already met, found that the source code was missing. This software program is hamstrung without it, but West found a trace signal matching the Perseus algorithms briefly emanating from a location in Mumbai. Just a blip that lasted less than a minute or so."

"India...that's where I tracked Cal to."

"The signal's appearance coincided with Cal's disappearance from the U.S., so, given his prior connection to Burke, I figured it had to be in his possession."

He leaned back, plucking a grainy photo from under a pile of papers on his desk then handing it to her. "A few days after that, we caught a break and picked up Cal on a security camera on the outskirts of Kolkata near the Bangladesh border. That's when Neil Patterson stepped in. He was confident that, if he could make contact with Cal, he could convince him to come in from the cold with the source code, though Neil had no way of getting in touch with him.

"Neil believed Viper was the key, since she had also gone off the grid at about the same time as all of this. He used a previous back-door channel from when she was with his search-and-destroy unit years ago and established contact, which led to him connecting with Shepard and setting everything in motion."

"It's good to hear that Cal hasn't been shouldering all of this in addition to everything else that has gone to hell in his life. But why not just bring him here with the source code? Why is he still on the run in India?"

"Burke had left specific instructions with Cal regarding a colleague in Mumbai who had helped him design the original source code and could properly configure it for integration into the mainframes here."

"I thought Burke had nearly completed Perseus before his death. Why does Cal need this woman's help in configuring it?"

"Good question...with a layered answer."

"I'd expect no less from you, Colonel."

There was a delay in his response as he shot a surprised look at her for the quick-witted comment. "West indicated that once the source code device gets accessed or there's any attempt to integrate it with the mainframes here, it would send out a signal...that same signal we used to locate Cal in the first place and that will paint a target on us here, alerting Begley to our location."

Foley stepped around the table, pointing to a group of

men on ladders in the northeast corner who were installing reflective steel plates on the ceiling. "Until this place is further hardened from digital intrusion and thermal scans, and until Cal can get the fully operational source code to us, our efforts with activating Perseus are on standby. Besides, if we did manage to bypass initial detection by inserting the unaltered source code that Cal has, we would most likely still need the help of this woman, Zemenova, to configure the damn thing, and she could be in the wind by then."

Vogel moved up to the map on the whiteboard. "There was a woman I came across with Cal recently, connected with an armed assault in the jungle northeast of Delhi. Is she the cyber expert you're referring to?"

"Yes, Theresa Zemenova, that's the former colleague of Burke's. She's the reason Cal went to that remote stretch in the first place after discovering a landline number she was using in a province he'd tracked her to last week. There wasn't much known about her. I think she has been operating under an alias for some time since we couldn't pull up anything on her, which is why Cal was keeping her pursuit low profile."

"And where's he at now?"

Foley raised his eyebrows, staring at her. "We just lost contact with him."

She narrowed her eyes. "You don't know where he is? I thought by what you just told me, you'd be providing support and intel, especially since Begley has to have a team of his own on Cal's trail."

Foley canted his head. "That's where you come in. You see, until recently, Cal was only checking in with me periodically since there was little for him to report about locating the woman. I did receive a call a few hours ago from him, indicating he required armed support at their exfil point near a town called Kablana, but he was supposed to check in with me already to let me know what he needed and when."

Foley leaned over, rotating his laptop around to show a map and satellite image of an apartment complex in south-central India.

"That was taken several hours ago outside the safe-house that Cal and Viper were using. There was an explosion in the northeast corner where their place was located."

She waved her hand at the other staff in the warehouse. "Again, why were they operating with a skeleton crew, handling a mission of this nature without any outside support?"

"He wasn't exactly alone all this time, but I can't get into all of the operational details right now. I do have some old agency assets in India, but frankly, it's uncertain how deep Begley's corruption runs within our clandestine units, so my usual support network is limited. Cal laid down the parameters, and he and Viper have been running their own show with funds and resources of mine passed along to them via Patterson."

He sat down in his chair. "The fact is, we need him. *I* need what he has in order to complete Perseus and make it fully operational. Think of what we can accomplish with that tool at our disposal, Lynn—far beyond what you and I were capable of doing under the restrictive auspices at Langley."

She frowned. "I don't know...we didn't have too many operational tethers at the agency or when you ran the SD units. It was more akin to the Wild West at times."

"And you were an instrumental part of that." He leaned forward, his piercing blue eyes seeming to stare through her.

"I hope you will re-up with me now. What do you say, Lynn?"

Vogel thought about what such unbridled power could do in the hands of a lesser man. She'd known Foley since beginning at Langley years ago and found his reputation within clandestine services as being *a chess-playing Pitbull.*

But she had also seen too many individuals in the upper echelons of the intelligence community become corrupted by power. She sensed that Foley was being forthright as always, and that provided some assurance, but her mind was still swirling from her very public humiliation at the agency and the violent aftermath of the assault on the van.

How do I go back to Langley even if Begley is put behind bars?

She knew the latter would never happen and the President would not and could not suffer the political blow of having someone as high-profile as Begley exposed for his corruption and treason at the head of the very intelligence agencies responsible for the nation's security.

Her career at Langley was in limbo, maybe over for good. She wasn't sure how she'd ever get her name cleared and command the respect of the people under her again—the very people who watched her get hauled off in handcuffs while Begley's thug verbally assailed her for treasonous crimes.

If she was to have a chance at all of restoring her reputation, it would be working with Foley, at least for now. She would have to sort out the rest as she went, but looking around at the other members in Foley's new unit and their budget-rich resources in the warehouse, Vogel felt some sense of relief that she would still be using her skills to serve the country and protect operators like Cal and Viper.

She took a deep breath, pulling her shoulders back. "I'll

help you find Cal, but my loyalty is as much to him as it is to you, and if the time ever comes when I am forced to choose, then we will have to revisit my role here."

"Fair enough." He stepped aside, motioning to a desk to his right that held an array of computer equipment before a large wall monitor. "I will leave you to work your magic. Just keep me posted and let me know when you find our boy."

———

"Talk to me," snapped Begley as he paced around Palermo's desk while the man continued scrolling through fresh surveillance and satellite footage.

The stout cyber guru leaned back, placing his hands behind his head and grinning as he nodded at his monitor. "Your ploy with the van worked. I got 'em!"

Begley leaned in closer, examining the Bell 205 helicopter that had landed a few minutes ago on the roof of a small building amidst a cluster of derelict warehouses on the outskirts of Baltimore.

He looked at the image of the man leading the others along the roof towards an elevator entrance. Begley enhanced the faces, his eyes zeroing in on one individual.

His heart raced, a wolfish grin creeping along his face. "Foley, I knew it. You rat-bastard. I have you now, old man."

38

NORTHERN DELHI

VICTOR FELT HIS IPHONE VIBRATE, his pulse quickening when he saw it was the head of the Orlov crime syndicate in Moscow instead of his usual handler.

"Yes, sir. How may I be of service?"

"I am sitting at my desk watching real-time satellite footage of the American you were pursuing fleeing from a tunnel below a burning building in south Delhi—the same American you reported interfering with your efforts to acquire the woman in the jungle yesterday."

"Fleeing from who?"

"Looks like an organized team of hitters. Regardless, he is with four other people, one of whom is the woman you were sent to snatch. Find them and find that stolen software before someone else gets their hands on it. I'm having my staff here relay you the coordinates of their last known location. They appear to be heading southwest on Highway 48."

"I will take care of him, sir, and obtain the stolen software."

"Good, because it's starting to feel like I am doing your job for you, and I have no use for redundant elements in my organization."

Victor heard the phone go silent, his mouth becoming dry as he anxiously scanned the new satellite images on his phone.

39

DOWNTOWN PHILADELPHIA

THE WEIGHT of the bulbous propane tanks caused Russ Buchanan to slow down as he carefully maneuvered the two-wheeled dolly down the chipped concrete steps onto the third and last level of the old stairwell. Behind him was his Sentinel boss, James Reynolds, who was struggling to move his heavily laden dolly.

Pausing at the bottom, Buchanan dragged his sleeve across his sweaty forehead then lowered the zipper on the center of the blue jumpsuit he'd stolen from the delivery company. He removed the bronze key on a piece of cord around his neck then inserted it into the lock on the steel door to his right.

"Why the hell couldn't there be an old service elevator down here?" said Reynolds, a barrel-chested man in a similar outfit.

"'Cause that'd be too easy, and we don't do easy, remember," said Buchanan. "Plus, when they built these old service tunnels for the subways back in the day, they had twelve-year-old workers to haul their shit."

Reynolds shook his head, snickering. "Then someone just had to go and ruin everything by passing those child labor laws."

Buchanan thrust his chin out at a young woman in a blue jumpsuit trotting down the steps, her athletic figure backlit by the dim light emanating from the topside entrance.

"Glad you could take time to make it," said Reynolds, giving her an irritated glance. "In the future, you show up on time so we're not the only ones doing all the heavy lifting. We've already done three trips down here."

"Yeah, well, Sentinel doesn't pay my bills. That's what my day job is for and, unfortunately, I got stuck at the tutoring center," said Nessa Hoffman, who was busy retying her long black hair into a tight ponytail.

Buchanan removed a small metallic flask of whiskey from his back pocket, taking a swig. "When Sentinel pulls this operation off tomorrow night, you can quit your gig and do this full-time, kiddo."

"Do what, exactly? What are we doing with all these propane tanks down here?" she said.

"You'll see," said Buchanan, who nodded at the open doorway.

Buchanan pulled three headlamps from his jumpsuit, handing one to Reynolds and Nessa then sliding the other onto his forehead. He leaned his dolly back, bracing the heavy weight, then both men continued pushing their payloads down the sloped corridor that led another hundred yards into a dome-shaped utility room. Their boots kicked up a fine layer of dust that caused Buchanan to start hacking as he fought to breathe in the stale air.

The dilapidated tunnels had once been part of a spur route for the present-day NRG subway that sliced through the heart of downtown. This particular passageway hadn't been used in years, and Buchanan had to spend time at the public library and city hall meticulously sifting through old maps and 1950s technical blueprints on microfiche to pinpoint the exact tunnel.

Buchanan white-knuckled the dolly to prevent it from running away on the incline, finally coming to a jolting stop when the floor leveled out in the utility room. He kept his headlamp trained on a narrow area of the room where thirty more propane tanks were situated next to a few dozen blue barrels of ammonium nitrate.

He cleared his throat, turning towards Nessa. "You got the stuff I asked for?"

She nodded, removing her backpack and pulling out a spool of heavy-duty 15-amp power cord, wire cutters and insulated electrician's gloves.

"This was everything on your list," she said, taking several steps back like the items were about to become animated.

"So, once you hook all this shit up, it's supposed to blow out the floor and collapse the subway tunnel, right?" said Reynolds.

Buchanan looked up from the items on the ground. "Except the subway doesn't quite run over this room. There's a large conference center two levels above us that will be filled with close to 5,000 people attending the consumer electronics show this week. Not to mention some of the most brilliant minds in computer design."

Reynolds and Nessa gave each other uneasy glances. "What, yeah, sure, Russ," snickered Reynolds.

Buchanan's face grew taut, his usual boyish grin fading.

"What are you talking about?" said Nessa, glancing back at the doorway. "We are just supposed to make a statement by shutting down the subway for a few months to draw attention to the city's corrupt transportation department."

"Plans change, darlin'," said Buchanan as he stood up, arching his back in a stretch. "And if there's one thing my time in the military taught me years ago, it's that there's nothing like a hefty bodycount to sway hearts and minds. It's a tactic that's been used since the Romans to win over the masses."

"This is a joke, right? What are you talking about?" said Nessa.

"Not this time, kiddo," said Buchanan.

"We're not murderers, and I didn't sign on for any of this shit," she said.

Nessa backed up, tripping on the edge of a faded canvas tarp covering what looked like crates, the scuffle from her boot pulling back the edge. She shrieked, hopping up, her hand stretching over her open mouth as she stared down at several pale bodies with bullet holes in their skulls.

"What the fuck's going on here?" said Reynolds, staring at several members from the Sentinel group.

"Oh my God," shouted Nessa.

"Just some contributors to the cause," said Buchanan, removing a suppressed .380 Bersa pistol from his pocket. "This is the part where I talk about how the blood of patriots and tyrants refreshes the tree of liberty and all that, but you already know the quote, since it's Sentinel's fucking mantra —one that nobody is really prepared to put into action."

Reynolds raised his hands. "Please, bro, this ain't you. You don't want to do this."

"I do actually, or nothing will change in this country. You

see, once this terrorist attack occurs, the public and the politicians will be so outraged that there wasn't a system in place to prevent insurgents like yourselves from doing something so heinous that they will gladly sign away their own personal rights to a higher power."

"Why the hell would you be a part of something like that? You sound like the fucking terrorist, Russ," said Reynolds.

"Create enough chaos and uncertainty in the average working stiff's daily grind and they will gladly sacrifice their rights in exchange for keeping their families safe. And I for one am tired of being part of a reactionary force that hunts down bad guys that we could have prevented from striking in the first place if we had more eyes in the sky. I spent years in special-ops slaving away overseas, and for what? To come back here to a country torn apart by the same kinds of extremist mentality I was spilling blood for in some shithole."

He sent the first round into Reynolds' forehead, dropping the big man onto the bare ground, then turned towards Nessa. "That ape was just another mindless cog in the system, but it's a shame a pretty and talented lady like you got tied up in this social reform bullshit. You could have probably gone on to be a professor or a scientist, making real change."

Her lips trembled as tears streamed down her face. "I thought you were my friend. What happened to you?"

"I tried to talk some sense into your head. It's why I invited you for coffee on several occasions, trying to sway you away from this kind of nonsense, but you wouldn't listen."

"Sounds like you have plenty of your own bullshit you've

bought into with your own demented cause. At least I'm not a cold-blooded murderer, you fuck."

"Murder is just another tool, my dear, and it's something I've always been good at after decades of counter-insurgency, though I take no pleasure in ending someone like yourself." He squeezed off a burst of rounds into her chest, watching her collapse back onto the canvas tarp.

Buchanan sighed, sliding back the safety on his pistol before tucking it away, his eyes watching Nessa's chest issue out its last exhale.

"Sorry, kiddo. It's not what I wanted."

He looked at the six other victims, all of whom came from middle-class America and had been staunch supporters of Sentinel since his boss Jason Begley had quietly begun funding the group through a shell corporation three years ago.

Removing his backpack, Buchanan pulled out a small case. Extracting two vials and accompanying Q-tips, he swabbed the mouths of Reynolds and Nessa then placed the samples into Plexiglas tubes, securing the rubberized gaskets on top.

Next, he tore open an alcohol prep pad, wiping down each of his victims' fingers. A small tin provided him with the clay-like black ink to press their fingertips into before rolling them onto small glass plates to obtain the prints. When he was done, he removed a specialized camera from his pack. Buchanan slowly waved the device's shutter before Nessa's right eye, recording an iris scan, then did the same to Reynolds, making sure to complete his task within the thirty-minute window after death needed to capture the iris' still active organic structure.

With the biometric data he'd collected from this small group, he would be able to provide Begley with a ghost crew of terrorists whose DNA signatures could turn up at future attacks around the country. Sentinel and its malevolent agenda would serve to fuel public outrage for years to come if necessary.

After he finished, he folded Nessa's slender arms across her chest then lowered her eyelids, removing the tarp from all the victims. Buchanan walked to the table, removing a particulate respirator that he slid over his face, then picked up a five-gallon bucket of powdered lime he'd placed there on a previous visit. He pried off the lid, pulling out a large scoop then liberally sprinkling the caustic compound onto the faces and hands of the victims to destroy the fingerprint and dental evidence. Between the massive explosion that was about to take place and the chemical eradication of the bodies, there would be little evidence left for recovery personnel to locate in the aftermath of the attack.

Buchanan emptied the remaining powder over the rest of the corpses then flung the bucket on the ground. He backed up, unzipping his backpack and retrieving four blocks of SEMTEX and a detonator, then he went to work assembling the IED components against the wall, forcing away the memory of the silenced souls behind him.

When he was done, he retraced his steps through the passage, locking the door then trotting up the stairwell to the street entrance. Before stepping outside, he felt his burner phone vibrating in his back pocket.

Answering, he heard Begley's voice, which was more frantic than usual. "I need you and a strike team on standby. Sending you coordinates to the location of Colonel Foley's operation in west Baltimore. How far out are you from that city?"

"About two hours driving time from Philly. I need

another twenty minutes to finish the relays for the IEDs here, then I can gather my team and be on our way."

"Good. Once you're in position near Foley's facility, contact me and I'll give you up-to-date intel on their setup." A pause followed, Begley's voice lowering. "And Buchanan, this is going to be a clean sweep...no survivors."

AFTER THEY REGROUPED outside the tunnels near the safe-house, Aden hotwired a weather-beaten Honda Civic, enabling the group to head towards the small town of Kablana, twenty miles southwest of Delhi.

A half-hour later, Viper slowed the vehicle, pulling off at the northern edge of the main street that ran east to west, and they all scanned the vehicles and pedestrians ahead.

"This is a very corrupt area from what I know, even for a small town. The Naja gang controls this region, and the police here are on their payroll," said Zemenova.

"Sounds like Afghanistan," said Viper as she glanced at Cal.

"Yeah, only then we had a Blackhawk nearby for a hasty exfil," he said.

Sayyid pointed to the end of the half-mile-long street at the west end where the forty-acre campus for a small community college was situated near the bridge leading to the small airfield. "Not much farther now."

Cal leaned in from the back seat, glancing at the side-walks and streets in either direction, his gut tightening at the sight of several parked trucks ahead with surly figures who clearly weren't locals.

"This place is already swarming with the Naja crew by the looks of it...and they're going to be searching for me. This is where I get out."

He motioned to a narrow alley to the right. "Drop Aden and me off over there, then the rest of you make your way to the other side of town while we keep my pals over here occupied. We'll plan to rendezvous at the community college." He inserted a comms device into his right ear then handed the other piece to Viper, who did the same.

She drove the car one block north, depositing Cal and Aden at the rear of a boarded-up two-story building whose rusted signage indicated it had once served as a medical clinic.

Cal grabbed a two-by-four from a pile of debris, smashing it into the handle on the back door. Swinging open the rickety door, he and Aden trotted up the stairwell, taking up shooting positions in the front windows.

Cal set his backpack down, unzipping it to have quick access to the six 30-round magazines for his MK12 rifle then sliding open the large windows while Aden did the same. Both men nervously watched Viper drive down the main street.

He knew there was a chance that one of the goons below could have been a part of Sai's group from the jungle preserve, in which case Zemenova might be recognized. His worries were soon confirmed when the vehicle was stopped three blocks later by a group of Naja gang members.

He glanced over at the other end of the room, seeing Aden's suppressed AR-10 already in position as if sensing Cal's thoughts.

Shepard removed a folding Defense Technologies

grenade launcher from his pack, loading a 37mm round into the barrel then snapping it shut. He stood up, bracing his left shoulder against the wall while directing the weapon at the battered truck closest to the four Naja gang members who were thirty yards from Viper's vehicle. He squeezed the trigger, and the grenade streaked out across the low rooftops below and struck the rear cab of the truck, which erupted into a ball of flame and twisted shrapnel.

The remaining members darted for cover, swinging their AKs up at the surrounding rooftops. While the gang members below were searching for the shooter, Cal reloaded the weapon, sending another grenade downrange into a second vehicle.

He dropped low, an incoming barrage of wild machinegun fire spraying the windowsill to his right. Cal exchanged weapons, picking up his suppressed MK12. He and Aden opened fire on the gang members in the street as the locals began fleeing.

The remaining throng of henchman on the surrounding streets didn't waste time in massing, a dozen of them running along the sidewalks towards the front of the medical clinic. Cal and Aden managed to pick off three men before the others ducked out of sight below the second-floor awning.

A moment later, Cal heard the glass door below being smashed open, followed by the trample of footfalls as the assaulters made their way up the steps in an all-out rush.

Aden sprang up, rushing to the stairwell and plucking two grenades off his vest then flinging them below.

"This way," yelled Cal, pointing to a large bay window on the east side of the room that he had tossed a chair through. Aden darted towards him, Cal sidestepping and shooting beyond the man as two thugs ran into the room.

Both bodies succumbed to the lead attack, their chests leaking out crimson fluid as more henchmen stepped over their limp figures.

"Go," shouted Cal. Aden stepped out onto the ledge, leaping onto some stacked crates below. Shepard fired off a burst of rounds then ducked behind the door frame as the men in the other room began firing wildly.

He removed a grenade, yanking out the pin and tossing it into the crowd. Immediately following the explosion, he swept his muzzle out, shooting two wounded Najas who were staggering onto their feet, then he emptied his remaining rounds into another man rushing in from the stairwell.

WITH THE FIRST vehicle explosion taking out three gang members and turning the streets into a warzone, Viper hit the accelerator, plowing over a Naja henchman in front of her then steering through a tangle of gas-powered rickshaws and food carts on the street as she maneuvered through downtown.

Three blocks later, her progress was halted as a flood of terrified villagers in their cars and motorcycles poured into the street, colliding with a truck inbound from the south.

She looked ahead, seeing no way through the chaotic chokepoint. Viper flung open her door, retrieving her backpack. She pulled down a brown shawl, concealing the MP7 rifle she had just slung on her shoulder.

"Let's go. It'll be quicker on foot, and we only have a quarter-mile to cover." She tried to make it sound within easy reach, but she knew from experience that such distances could easily turn into a hellacious death march through a chaotic battlefield.

Sayyid and Zemenova followed alongside her, blending in with the other harried pedestrians scrambling around the damaged vehicles.

If it wasn't for their height, she might not have even noticed the four men who exited the large truck that had caused the traffic jam, their gazes fixed on Zemenova.

"Shit, we've got company," said Viper.

"Those are the guys who attacked the bus at the tiger preserve," whispered Zemenova, her face turning ashen as the men began closing the forty-yard distance between them.

"Get her to the college," snapped Viper to Sayyid as she flung back her shawl, raising up her MP7 and shooting the first Russian in the face then darting behind a delivery van as 7.62 rounds struck the vehicle.

Sayyid and Zemenova crouched low, maneuvering through the unoccupied cars clogging the main artery of town.

Viper glanced to her left, spotting an Anglo man who had just taken up a shooting position on a rooftop to the north, his gaze focused on Sayyid. She fixed her weapon sights on the sniper, pacing her breathing then squeezing off a round that splintered apart the right side of his skull. She quickly shuffled around the rear of the van, pausing to glimpse at the two remaining Russians bounding towards her position.

Viper backed up a foot, lying on her left side and directing her rifle muzzle under the van. A second later, a sliver of the men's leg movements was visible beneath a car twenty feet away. She fired a burst of rounds into the nearest man's ankles then swept her weapon to the right, executing the same motion on the other killer as both men toppled to the pavement. Viper finished off each one with another burst to their ribcages then hopped to her feet, crouch-running down the street.

She never saw the other henchman until it was too late. The burly thug rushed out from an alleyway and slammed into her side. She felt her ribs compress, her other side smashing into a rickshaw. The man kept his meaty hands pressed against her MP7, making it impossible to move.

Viper straightened up, driving the heel of her boot down on his instep then thrusting a spear-hand into the side of his trachea. He shuffled back, gagging but still gripping her rifle. Her right hand let go, and she removed her Glock and squeezed off three rounds into his face and neck before shoving him onto the hood of a car and scanning for other threats.

41

Rohan Patel stood on top of a five-story building on the south end of Kablana, his binoculars focused on a plume of smoke from burning vehicles near the downtown strip. His eyes traced the movement of two men exiting the old medical clinic on the east side of town. A vein in Patel's neck began throbbing as the bearded American filled his vision.

He heard his radio crackle with the frantic voice of his Najas reporting about two women and a man who'd just fled the scene where their vehicles suffered a rocket attack.

"Bring me my sniper rifle," he shouted at the stout man to his right. "And get more of our guys to the road that leads to the airfield. Block if off by whatever means necessary. That's where the other three must be heading."

The twelve-hour flight to Delhi felt like it took a week. Nolan was met at a military airstrip outside of the city by a six-man team of Special Frontier Force operators, members of India's Intelligence Bureau and counter-terrorism experts whose director had close ties with Colonel Foley.

As Nolan slid his weapons crate into the helicopter beside the other operators, he hoped he would be in time to make a difference in the battle he knew was unfolding thirty miles to the southwest as Vogel fed him real-time intel on the bloody conflict.

Cal Shepard operating his own Wild West show out here. Sounds like the guy Foley told me about.

He climbed into the cabin, sliding the door closed then buckling in as he glanced around at the other men. "I'll make this brief. I'm Derrick Nolan with the Critical Response Team, led by Ryan Foley, whom some of you have worked with before. We are heading to Kablana, where a team of our operatives are pinned down by three other opposing groups of hostiles. We need to clear a path to my colleagues on the ground so we can secure a package in their possession and get them the hell out of there."

Seems pretty straightforward...except for all the international laws about to be broken and the coming bodycount.

Viper bounded between vehicles for another block then sprinted into the lobby of the college admissions building, squatting next to Sayyid and Zemenova.

She glanced to the north, seeing a bulldozer smashing vehicles and food carts into a mangled mess that cut off passage across the bridge leading to the airfield.

"It's going to be suicide to head that way now. There are too many of those guys," Zemenova said.

"Good thing that's not where we're going," said Viper. She grabbed Zemenova's arm, leading her further inside the one-story building as Sayyid provided rear cover.

CAL AND ADEN sprinted between wrecked cars along the main street, pausing beside an overturned tea kiosk. He tapped on his ear-mic, contacting Viper.

"We're three blocks over at the college, but we're about to be met with heavy resistance. How soon can you get here?" she said.

He sensed it was a plea more than a question, her voice betraying a rare trepidation he'd only heard in battle a few other times.

"On my way, we are..."

Strafing bullets zippered along the kiosk, splintering wood off into his neck. He ducked down lower, feeling a burning sensation in his left shoulder where a round had torn through the edge of his bicep.

Fuck!

Cal fought to dismiss the pain, peering around the side of the three-foot-high cart at the four men advancing on his position.

Same dudes who stormed our safehouse.

He leaned back, using hand motions to Aden to indicate

his hasty plan. Aden nodded, getting into position on his belly and firing a single round into the small gas tank of a three-wheeled rickshaw. The explosion blew out the front of the rig, instantly killing one of the men in a storm of metal shrapnel and flame.

Cal sprang up on one knee, squeezing off three rounds at the nearest man, twenty yards away, catching him in the trachea and chin. Shepard dropped out his nearly spent magazine, replaced it with another thirty-rounder then racked the slide.

He heard the clanking of metal on the ground and saw a grenade land six feet away near a fire hydrant.

Oh, shit!

Cal flung himself back, scrunching up in a ball behind the kiosk and drawing his arms up around his head.

He felt the pavement rumble, seeing chips of concrete and steel blast into the walls of the pharmacy next to him followed by a geyser of water raining down on the street.

Aden was on his side, groaning and clutching his groin area, but Cal didn't see copious amounts of blood, which gave him some measure of hope that the shrapnel hadn't struck the femorals. Cal heard the other men in the assault team backing up. He peered around the corner of the kiosk, wondering why they were retreating when they clearly had the tactical advantage.

"SAY AGAIN," said Bishop into his ear-mic as Palermo relayed satellite intel on Kablana. He raised his fist, telling his remaining men to cease fire as they held their positions behind the derelict vehicles. The grenade he'd just tossed in Shepard's direction had either killed the two men by the kiosk or disabled them enough so they weren't an immediate threat.

"I said, that woman that was with Shepard's group is at a college building three blocks from your location. They must be trying to get to that airfield and escape, as you originally suspected."

Fucking Shepard. I'll come back for you later.

He grit his teeth, motioning to his remaining mercs to follow him.

CAL DUCK-WALKED OVER TO ADEN, helping the man to lean against the tire of the car. The wound in the man's upper thigh had just missed the femoral, and Cal tore open the top of his trauma kit, removing a package of QuikClot and a triangle bandage, wrapping the bloody gash.

"No more dancing for a while, alright," he said, helping the man up.

They hadn't moved more than ten feet when the air shattered around Cal's head, the sickening sound of a high-caliber round zinging past him and penetrating the brick storefront behind him.

He lowered Aden, both men resuming their prone positions as he searched the nearby rooftops for the sniper.

He heard his earpiece crackle, the sound of the frequency suddenly changing. "Raptor, this is Bird-Dog. The sniper is three hundred yards to the south on the roof of a five-story building, so just stay where you're at for now."

Cal felt time moving in slow motion as he struggled to process the voice. The woman's familiar tone ushered in a flood of memories from other harrowing battles in foreign lands. His eyes darted along the glittering glass shards on the ground, and he wondered if he was hallucinating.

"Lynn, is that...is that really you?"

"I've got you, Cal. I'm working with Colonel Foley, and right now, I need you to stay put then do as I say when I say it, copy?"

He felt his heart racing as much from the gunfight as from the thrill of hearing Vogel's voice. "Loud and clear."

"When I tell you to, you need to run like hell for the corner store across from you."

"ONE MORE SHOT and I'll have a fix," said Nolan to Vogel as he lay prone beside the smokestack on the roof of a porcelain factory eight hundred yards distant from the sniper's last known position.

"You'll have it, but make it count. We may not get another chance like this."

"Copy that." Nolan focused the scope of his M24 rifle on the general location where he knew the sniper was located, figuring the shooter must be positioned behind the low brick border surrounding the rooftop of a lime-processing facility.

He heard his earpiece go silent for a moment, knowing Vogel had just switched channels, giving Shepard the order to run.

Then he saw it—a brief but tantalizing flash of light emanating from a small gap in the bricks on the northeast corner of the building. Nolan steadied his breathing, his body oblivious to the discomfort of the hot asphalt roof and the hungry flies ravaging his face. There was only the singular task ahead.

The M24 barked out, its .338 round punching through the gap in the brickwork and into the yielding bone and flesh on the other side, spraying Patel's head onto the roof.

Nolan racked the bolt, chambering a new round and squeezing off another projectile that tore into the upper pec of a henchman who had just sprung up to run.

"Excellent work, Nolan. Shepard is in the clear and is heading north."

"Affirmative. I'll be done here shortly, then I'll rendezvous with him, so let him know I'm inbound."

Nolan sent three more rounds successfully downrange into the fleeing men getting choked up at the stairwell entrance. When the distant rooftop was devoid of movement, he slowly crawled back behind the concrete smokestack then stood up, slinging his rifle and removing his Glock before trotting down the rear fire escape to the rest of the Special Frontier Force operators securing the alleyways.

44

"Viper, you have close to twenty tangos moving towards your location from the west as well as three others from the east, do you copy?" said Vogel in her earpiece, responding to Vogel's update.

"Affirmative. Where's Cal?" She squatted down amidst the overturned vending machines and food carts she'd used as a barricade before the shattered lobby doors in the college admissions building.

"He's on his way. The man with him is injured, but Cal said it's manageable."

"Aden...what happened?" The words seemed stuck in her throat.

"Grenade went off. Those three guys heading your way were engaging them and, by the way they move, they're probably Begley's strike team."

She scowled. "Begley...how I'd like to soften his face with my boots."

"You and me both," said Vogel.

Viper leaned inside the building, shouting up towards

the roof hatch where Sayyid was located. "Talk to me. What's happening?"

"Right now, we've got movement at the front and on the east side. There's no way out of here other than heading through the building behind us then through the backside of campus, but that'll just lead us into an alley that doesn't look like it has much cover.

Viper tapped on her earpiece again. "Hey, Bird-Dog, any chance you can call in a drone strike? That'd sure be welcome right now."

"Uhm, agreed. I'm not sure the colonel has access to those capabilities."

"You mean, *yet*." She watched a group of Patel's henchmen moving in and spreading out between the first row of abandoned cars within a hundred yards of the campus.

"So, Lynn, when did you sign on with the colonel?" She needed to calm her nerves, and Vogel's voice was just the solution, as it had been with her on numerous missions abroad—a lifeline back to the world of the living and the country whose shores she yearned for.

"I just kind of walked into things in the past few hours or so."

She steadied the barrel of her MP7, squeezing off two rounds into the head of a tall thug trotting towards the sidewalk to the left.

"Sounds like the way Foley usually recruits his staff. Did he just waltz into your office with a tempting proposal you couldn't resist?" She swung her weapon to the right, shooting another man in the neck as he peered out from the rear bumper of a taxi.

"Waltz is too kind a word. The image that comes to mind

is more like one of those Viking battering rams you see in the movies."

She leaned back, seeing two gunmen peek out from their concealed positions behind a cement guardrail, strafing the admissions building with a wild barrage. "Yeah, he can be like that. Sometimes, I think that's where Cal gets his bullheaded approach to solving problems."

"I gotta cut out for a minute, Viper. I'll be back shortly."

"Always good to hear from you, Lynn." She removed a grenade from her pack, pulling the pin and flinging it towards a small bus where four men were concealed.

45

Bishop paused before the corner of a pharmacy, glancing around the edge at the burning vehicles and shattered storefronts two blocks from the college.

He heard Palermo's tinny voice in his earpiece. "I'm pretty sure that the group at the college is waiting for Shepard and his pal to arrive so they can make a beeline for the airfield. There's one plane on that runway. It has to be their way out."

Bishop lowered his ballcap to cut the glare on the glass-riddled streets, seeing one of his men point ahead at the twin-engine Cessna on the airfield across the ravine, a quarter-mile from their location.

"Screw this," Bishop said, setting his pack down and removing a LAWs rocket. "I'll take out their goddamn ride then finish them off one by one."

He trotted down the sidewalk, keeping low as he and his two men made their way to the alley behind a run-down motel. Bishop needed to clear a delivery truck parked near a grocery store's loading ramp before he could get a clear shot of the plane. Rounding the front bumper of the vehicle, he heard a dull thwack followed by a groan. The operator behind him collapsed, part of his jaw and nose missing.

Bishop darted forward, ducking around the other side of the truck. The other man behind him took a round to his cervical region and dropped to the pavement with a thud.

Bishop slung the LAWs rocket, removing his Galil rifle while tapping on his ear-mic. "What the fuck's going on? Did you see where that came from?"

"Sniper at your six," said Palermo.

"No shit, asshole. Give me an exact location."

"Hang on." Palermo's ragged breathing filled Bishop's ear-mic. A second later Palermo barked excitedly as if he was there in the alley, but Bishop knew that the closest the pudgy computer whiz got to a firearm was on his Xbox. "Three hostiles. Third-floor window of the office building two blocks east of you."

He looked down at his dead men, seeing the precision kill shots. "These wasn't a local, so who is it?"

"Just got a match from a face I scanned on the street earlier...looks to be Victor Udinov, a heavy hitter for the Orlov crime syndicate out of Moscow. Must be the same guys you ID'd earlier by that tiger preserve."

This town's a fucking shooting gallery. I need to get this job over with already.

He heard Begley's voice break in. "Take out the plane so no one can escape with the source code, then eliminate Shepard and his crew."

"I don't have a clear shot yet on the plane."

"Then *get* a clear shot. Time is running out. I need that source code removed from the playing field, now, before the attack in Philly!"

Bishop crept forward a foot, peering at the tail section of the plane, which was partly visible. It would be a challenge to guarantee a direct hit at this range, and he knew his head would be vaporized if he ventured a foot beyond the truck.

"Two minutes and it'll be done." He tapped off his ear-mic, not wanting to hear Begley's voice again until this contract was over.

Bishop leaned his Galil against the front tire, removing a smoke grenade from his vest and tossing it into the street near the office complex, then he removed the LAWs rocket slung on his shoulder. He counted to five until the smoke had dispersed enough, quickly sliding the LAWs onto the front bumper of the truck, aiming it then depressing the trigger. The rocket tore into the third-floor window in a deafening explosion of flames amidst body parts raining down on the street.

Bishop quickly grabbed his Galil, trotting down the alley until he reached the west end of town behind the community college campus. He dropped his backpack onto a low wall then rested the barrel of his rifle on top, squatting down and sighting in the Cessna.

He estimated it was roughly 1,400 feet to the target, pushing the Galil's upper range for a destructive shot.

Bishop wiped his sweaty brow, steadying his breathing, then leaned forward, welding his cheek against the stock like he'd done a thousand times before. He adjusted his rifle scope for windage and elevation then centered the red dot on the frame near the left propeller.

Squeezing the trigger, he saw a flutter of metal shear off. Methodically, he repeated the same motion, draining four more rounds until he saw black smoke sputtering out from the propeller engine. For good measure, he refocused his sights on the front tire and punched several rounds into the rubber with his remaining rounds. He left the depleted Galil leaning against the wall before removing his Beretta pistol.

He shouldered his backpack then turned his gaze towards the staccato of gunfire erupting on the other side of the tiny campus. He figured he would first have to punch through a few gang members enroute to the rear of the admissions building where Palermo had indicated Shepard's team was at, but he had a few pistol mags left that he hoped would be sufficient to complete the final leg of his mission.

If not, then I've still got one more ace up my fuckin' sleeve.

46

CAL HAD HASTILY SWATHED his bullet-grazed bicep in a bandanna then managed a half-trot, holding Aden up with one arm while keeping his pistol at a low-ready as they made their way down an alley to the north that ran parallel to the main street.

He wasn't sure if any of the residents were left in the town, and he regretted that a small war had been brought to their doorstep. He thought about how many places and battles he'd been in abroad in villages just like this only to be whisked off in a helicopter back to a forward operating base with showers, cold beer and a stocked chow hall while the villagers picked up the pieces of their shattered lives.

Right now, he was just focused on getting Aden to safety and rendezvousing with the others. It felt like the main battlefield was behind them, but he was sure there would be more Najas or some of Bishop's crew to contend with on the streets ahead.

Cal came to the end of the alley, setting Aden against the brick wall of a motel then scanning the route in every direction. Two blocks away was the college, whose location was easily identified by the barrage of gunfire emanating from the streets out front.

Viper had indicated earlier that the only way in was through a narrow entrance at the rear, between two science buildings and a greenhouse, since all of the Naja guys were situated on the opposite end of campus.

"You good for another jog around the neighborhood?" he said, hoisting Aden up, not expecting an answer from the groaning figure, who just gave a weak thumbs-up.

They made it to the next block, hobbling to the edge of a campus science building. Cal set the man down near a dumpster. Immediately, he caught a blur of movement to his right. He swung his Glock up to see Nolan trotting to a halt, the operator lowering his M24 rifle while raising up a gloved hand.

"Whoa, easy, fella. Derrick Nolan."

"Yeah, I figured. Vogel said you were on the way. One of Foley's guys, eh?" Cal shot his thumb in the direction of the medical clinic. "With that sniper shot you made, it looks like you have some passable skills with a firearm, so that's good."

Nolan's eyes narrowed. "Shit, I was bagging rabbits with a .22 when I was eight years old, so I've probably got more trigger time than you, Ace."

"Cardboard figures at the county fair don't count, but if Foley singled you out for his team, then that's sayin' something."

Nolan shook his head. "Foley and Vogel said you were uptight as hell."

"Why am I not surprised she's running with Foley?"

"Yeah, she was on the recruitment fast-track as of yesterday when Foley snatched her away from some mercs taking her to a black site."

"What? Why?"

"Jason Begley. He was coercing her into tracking you down, threatening her family. His goons were hauling her off to the woods until Foley showed up."

Shepard felt his pulse quicken at the thought of Begley pawing into Vogel's life to reach him, but he felt relieved that she was safe, marveling at the colonel's reach.

Looks like the old man's dream team of shit-hot operators is fully operational. Thank God Lynn is there with him.

Both men turned, seeing a glimmer of movement near a waist-high concrete wall by the side of the college campus. Before they could react, the leader of Begley's strike team darted out of sight between buildings.

Cal nodded at Aden. "Nolan here has graciously volunteered to get you inside with Viper and the others."

He clutched his Glock 17 tighter, trotting off. "I've got one more loose end to take care of."

Cal increased his speed to a sprint, heading past a shed then coming to a stop near the corner. Peering around the edge, he caught the silver glint of a knife in the sun as it rushed at his chest. Cal pivoted slightly as Bishop's blade made purchase on his left forearm. He dropped his pistol, immediately parrying the next thrust then smashing a right backhand into the man's nose. Bishop backpedaled, blood leaking down over his lips as he made a wild slash that nearly caught Cal on the shoulder.

Shepard sidestepped, removing his six-inch blade as both men circled each other. He was sore and running on an empty tank from days of being on the go. He knew he would be relying on sheer reflex from years of blade and combatives training. He also knew that a skilled mercenary like the guy across from him was probably operating in a similar fashion, and now it would either come down to whether Shepard could reacquire his pistol or whether he was more adept with his carving abilities than his opponent.

Cal feinted high towards Bishop's head then dropped his blade hand enough to snipe the man's abdomen with the tip. A narrow rivulet of crimson leaked out from the tiny laceration, but it wasn't enough to prevent Bishop from lunging at him with a deceptively low thrust that nicked Cal on the hip.

Shepard recognized a subtle Indonesian Silat move unfamiliar to most military combatives guys.

"Too bad you're gonna die far from home, Shepard—you and your pals." He nodded towards a twenty-foot-long propane tank against the back wall of the first building where Viper and the others were located. Attached to the tubular steel was a strip of door-breaching SEMTEX and a timer.

No, no, shit!

Cal tried to circle to the right as Bishop lunged at him again with a quick flurry of slashes. Shepard evaded to the left then pivoted slightly, avoiding the blade strikes, never seeing the dirt being kicked up into his face by the man's left foot.

Cal knew the killshot that was coming next, most likely aimed at his throat. He ran to the left, thrashing his knife while trying to shake his head and clear his vision. All he saw was a blur heading at his face. Instinctively, his left parrying hand shot up, intercepting the man's strike while countering with a single thrust that stuck deep into Bishop's lower abs. The man squealed in pain, backing up and clutching his belly as intestines began spilling into his hand.

Shepard brushed his fingers along his eyelids, the tears having flushed out enough dust for him to see more clearly. He advanced, sending a vicious shin kick into the side of

Bishop's right knee. The cartilage popped, and the man collapsed on his side. Cal stomped on the man's wrist, breaking the bones then kicking away the blade. He leaned over, pulling out Bishop's pistol and flinging it in the bushes.

Cal turned and bolted for the propane tank, yanking off the sticky cord of SEMTEX and then plucking out the timer, which was down to single digits. He walked back towards Bishop, whose blue innards were continuing to unspool on the lawn.

The man gave a bronchial laugh, pointing towards the airfield. "Your plane...I killed it. You're fucked. There's no way out of here now, and soon all those skinnies out front will overrun your pathetic band of misfits."

Cal nodded towards the large college banner draped on the building as Bishop sputtered out his last few breaths.

ITAE

Institute of Technology and Engineering

"The airfield was never the goal."

THERESA ZEMENOVA HAD few fingernails left to chew on as she watched the remaining numeric figures on the upload screen. Her laptop was routing the Perseus source code through a secure portal she had established using the college's sizeable mainframes.

"Thirty seconds then we'll be done here," she said to Sayyid, who stood in the doorway of the room with his weapon trained on the hallway entrance.

A sudden increase in gunfire from the north followed by multiple grenade blasts tore through the streets in front of the admissions building. Sayyid waited a moment then peered out the window, seeing a team of Indian commandos surgically eliminating the remaining Naja gang members.

He swung his AK towards a rush of footfalls from the hallway, then relaxed as Viper announced her approach.

She entered the room, the barrel of her MP7 still smoking.

"Well?" she said, staring wide-eyed at Zemenova.

The woman leaned back in her chair, her shoulders slouching. "I think Cal owes me a cold beer or two."

Viper moved up to the laptop, seeing the completed upload indicator and grinning. "A brewery of your own is more like it."

47

Maryland

CAMP DAVID PRESIDENTIAL **Retreat**

JUST WHEN RYAN FOLEY thought he'd descended the third and last flight of stairs under the east entrance of the countryside retreat, the Secret Service agent paused before a small steel door and unlocked it, ushering him down yet another flight of steps. The concrete walls were chipped and unpainted, and a musty odor permeated the air.

At the bottom, the man unlocked another door, flicking on a light switch in the ten-by-twenty storage room. The agent motioned for him to enter then closed the door.

Foley's eyes swept around the museum-like atmosphere, which contained an assortment of old furniture, crates of LP records and dust-covered wine bottles lining a bookshelf. To his right was an antique cherry desk whose border was inlaid with a narrow ribbon of turquoise that snaked towards the far right corner, where the initials "TR" were ornately etched. He ran his fingers over the letters.

"Damn, Teddy. It would have been an honor to serve under you, sir."

The door at the other end of the room opened, and President Nathan Weller casually entered. The man was dressed in slacks with a blue wool sweater, the most unassuming outfit Foley had ever seen in him.

"Don't look so surprised, Ryan. I only get to shake the suit and tie about once a month, so I have to..."

Foley extended his hand, both men shaking. Weller moved to the bookcase, sliding aside weathered original editions of *The Tempest* and *Hamlet* then pulling out a small cigar humidor resting on its side.

He unclasped the latch, opening it and pulling out two cigars. He handed one to Foley, who looked at it like it was dipped in gold.

"Are these what I think they are?"

Weller flared an eyebrow. "Yep. Gurkha Black Dragons. $1,150 a cigar and extremely hard to find."

Weller prepped the cigar then removed the monogrammed gold Zippo from the box and lit his stogie, handing the lighter to Foley.

"Not sure if I should smoke it or store it away under glass."

Weller exhaled, a satisfied expression sliding over his face. "There are no smoke alarms down here, so light up. This is where I come when I need a few minutes away from the chaos up top...not to mention the First Lady doesn't approve."

Foley partook of the cigar, enjoying the spicy aroma that had a pleasant buttery aftertaste.

"I know you are a busy man, but I requested this

meeting in person as there's something regarding one of your own staff that I have to discuss with you."

"My staff?"

"Yes, sir. My team has uncovered a plot for a domestically driven terrorist attack here on U.S. soil in the next few days. We are still trying to determine the precise location, but our intel indicates that the assault is being spearheaded by an off-the-books group funded by Jason Begley."

Weller's eyes widened. "My director of national intelligence...that Jason Begley?"

"I'm afraid so, sir. I have recordings of him meeting with Senator Nicholas Edgeworth, who is in league with him to re-allocate funds from our other shadow agencies to serve Begley's efforts."

Weller rubbed the back of his neck, pacing the room then putting out his cigar in a used ashtray on the bookshelf. "You're a hundred percent sure on this? He's the head of all our clandestine agencies, for Christ's sake."

"I am, sir." Foley removed a silver flash-drive from his pocket, handing it to the President. "We have authenticated audio of Begley and Edgeworth as well as evidence that Begley has a designated black site of his own on the outskirts of Arlington, where I believe he has a device similar to Perseus, given the nearly identical electronic signals and energy output coming from that location."

Weller clutched the flash-drive, his face reddening. "That son of a bitch. He was assigned by my predecessor but has always seemed like he was more than capable in his job. I would never have expected something on this scale from someone in such a critical role in my administration."

The President leaned back against the antique desk. "I can have him arrested within the hour."

"Sir, I've gamed this out from several angles, and right now I need him to think that he's off the radar until I can pinpoint the location of the attack. Picking him or his staff up off the streets now will surely trigger safeguards he has in place before we can identify his target."

"Ryan, you know my thoughts on dealing with terrorists. It's why I sanctioned you to create your unit. If this bastard needs to be taken down, then there'll be no hesitation on my end when the time comes...now or later."

He appreciated the man's candor and resolve. Having served as a combat pilot during the Gulf War before taking up public service, he knew Weller was a principled man who lived by a code not dissimilar to Foley's. But the colonel's job now was to both stop an attack on American soil and to minimize the political fallout on Weller's presidency. Any leaks to the media about Begley's treason would have a devastating ripple effect amongst allied intelligence agencies and undermine confidence in Weller's political image abroad and at home.

"I will take care of Begley and see to it that there's no blowback to you. I have a team inbound to India as we speak as part of a mission unfolding on those shores with a former operative of mine who has been working deep cover. He is in possession of a critical piece of software that could make or break this whole effort."

There was a pregnant silence in the air. Weller planted his feet firmly, staring at Foley.

"What else do you need from me?" He canted his head, staring at Foley, who had a surprised expression. "Ryan, I've made my living reading people. Not necessarily on the battlefield like yourself, but in the depraved jungle of D.C. Why else did you want to meet with me?"

Foley tamped out his cigar in the ashtray. "I have one request, sir. My operative in India has been on the run for nearly a month. He's being targeted by Begley and our intel agencies here for crimes he didn't commit. He was one of my own and served with distinction for years in my search-and-destroy unit. His name is Cal Shepard, and he has sacrificed more for this country than the world will ever know, both personally and professionally."

Weller's eyes darted along the wall. "Shepard...why do I know that name?"

"He was all over the news during the summer after someone leaked his name as a CIA agent and fabricated his involvement in the death of Stephen Burke and his staff."

Foley pulled his shoulders further back. "Sir, Shepard lost his own wife and unborn daughter during that explosion at Burke's estate and has been a hunted fugitive ever since. Begley has ramrodded any internal or public investigations into what happened, probably wanting Shepard for the fall guy to cover up his own side-mission if things go sideways. I am requesting that you grant a presidential pardon to a man who has given so much to this country and has walked away with so little for his service."

He glanced down at Weller's hand. "I've included the unredacted files of Shepard's time with the Special Activities Division on the flash-drive. It also covers the events that unfolded in the hours and days surrounding Burke's death."

He could see the man mulling over the information. The betrayal of one of his top-tier intelligence directors and the request to pardon a publicly known fugitive who was painted as a traitor to the agency was a lot to fathom.

Weller tucked the flash-drive into his pocket then extended his hand to Foley. "Thank you, Ryan, for being one of a very small handful of people in the world who has always had my back."

He headed to the door, pausing before opening it and looking back. "Keep me posted on Begley's undertakings. As for Shepard...he gets this current crisis resolved, he will have that pardon."

48

ONE HOUR Later

CAL and the others retreated to the outskirts of Kablana as the town was inundated with fire-trucks and first responders coming down from the larger cities to the north.

He sat in the back of an open van he'd commandeered for their ride out of Kablana, the two Syrian men and Zemenova resting under the shade of a large banyan tree along a seldom-used dirt road while Sayyid treated his friend's leg wound.

Cal looked over at Nolan, who was busy talking to the Indian commandos near their helicopter.

"Guess he's with Foley's new team," she said, putting the last series of Steri-strips on his knife wounds. "Glad of it, too."

"Yeah, he's alright. Not as good a shot as you or me though."

Viper chuckled, nudging him with her elbow. "Envious, Cal?"

"Pff...just making an observation."

"You were always Foley's and Patterson's all-star shooter."

He shook his head. "Damn right, girl. Best remember that too."

She wrapped her arm around his shoulder. "I don't think you have to worry about anyone ever replacing you."

Cal stood up, his bruised ribs aching. He removed his burner phone, seeing a phone number that, for once, he was relieved to answer.

"We're good to go, sir," he said.

"Excellent. Everything is underway here," said Colonel Foley. "You've had a helluva ride, son, being in the wind like this, and for too long. Now, we'll take it from here, Cal."

"And the source code?"

"Received and inserted into our mainframes back where it belongs thanks to Zemenova's work. It's been collating all the data and intel related to Begley, Edgeworth and any anomalies connected to their daily patterns, missing persons and business undertakings. So far, a large explosive device and a mass grave have been located by my contacts at the FBI beneath an old subway relay station in downtown Philly. Perseus indicated that the site was staged by a former private military contractor used by Begley in the past. We think the target was the consumer electronics conference, which would have taken out quite a chunk of his competition. We're still searching for other sites that he may have targeted."

"Wait, Senator Edgeworth?" said Cal, sifting through the details. "He's involved in this shit-show?"

"Afraid so."

Cal heard a man speaking in the background, indicating something about Phase II being ready to initiate.

"I'll catch up with you later, Cal. Right now, I've got something urgent to deal with, but just know, we would have never gotten this far without all you've done behind the scenes."

"Stay safe, Colonel."

The phone went silent. He was relieved his end of the mission was over, but a part of him wished he was back alongside Foley to witness the culmination of the battle that he knew was about to unfold from the fruits of his efforts in this country.

FOLEY STOOD over West's shoulder, watching the man tracing his slender finger along a red line extending on the map from southern India towards the United States East Coast.

"The malware that Viper obtained and that the woman calibrated was directed at the electrical relay station an hour ago."

West looked at the top-right corner of his screen, watching the numeric countdown begin, then glanced back at Foley.

"It's go-time, sir. The protective relay in Magellan's offsite power source will be flipped off briefly, allowing a power surge from outlying grids in the city to flood into the main conduit powering Begley's mainframes."

"Killing Magellan before it can ever awaken," whispered Foley as he stared at the digital battleground on the monitor.

"Sir, this will be more than just shutting down that system. It's going to be Pompeii over there."

Foley's face grew taut as he considered the radical shift

in his own thinking. After a lifetime of warfare abroad, his enemy's might was now determined by a single keystroke. He was witnessing firsthand that cyber superiority had tilted the scales away from ground wars.

He rested his hand on West's shoulder, seeing a row of black-and-white monitors illuminating to the left as a group of heavily armed operators began moving into the west end of their facility.

49

Russ Buchanan and his eight-man team of mercenaries were huddled in a white delivery van across from Foley's headquarters on the outskirts of downtown Baltimore. After several years of working undercover within Sentinel, it felt good to be back with a team of seasoned contractors like himself.

All of them were wearing body armor and helmet-mounted cameras and were equipped with enough weaponry to storm a small fortress, which was what he expected this would be. Buchanan sat in the chair, his eyes darting between the three computer monitors that were relaying a mixture of satellite and drone footage of the exterior of the warehouse.

"Sending you the infra-red scan from the interior now," said Palermo into his earpiece. "Looks like about fourteen personnel inside and quite a setup with the computer mainframes on the lower level."

Buchanan tapped his finger on the right monitor near the location of a set of stairs that led to a vault-like door on the second sub-level. "Getting to that point is our objective, but there are probably plenty of security cameras and armed guards on that first level, so we need to blitz in there and hit 'em hard before they can delete any of their software or destroy their computers."

"And Foley?" said a burly operator to Buchanan's right. "Dead or alive?"

Begley cut into their comms. "Not only dead, but I want his fucking skull filled with so much lead that no forensics guy on Earth will ever be able to reconstruct his head."

Buchanan clicked off his ear-mic, glancing to the operators on either side. "You heard the man. We take down everyone inside."

Buchanan tossed in two flash-bangs then waited three second before storming inside. He swept his rifle to the left, squeezing off three rounds into a female near a mainframe. He was surprised she was still standing after the effects of the flash-bangs, and his rounds had no effect, as she continued moving about the computers.

He heard his other men briefly firing at other targets then suddenly stopping. Buchanan removed his finger from his rifle trigger, staring up at the gray smoke fluttering along the shaft of colored light emanating from several high-def cameras mounted in parallel rows along the ceiling. He glanced back at the woman, whose image had just grown clearer with the dissipating smoke, her movements identical to when he entered the room.

"What the fuck's going on?" said his second-in-command, waving his hand through the lifelike image of a man in a white lab coat working on his tablet.

Buchanan tapped on his ear-mic. "You seeing this?"

"I can't make it out all that well. We've got some interference," said Begley. "What's happening?"

Buchanan stepped through one of the holographic

workers, tapping his hand on a large wooden crate near the corner to see if it was real.

He lifted the lid, seeing an arrangement of SEMTEX, the timer finishing its countdown with only five seconds left.

He lowered his rifle, shaking his head in resignation. "Checkmate by Foley."

50

BEGLEY'S MOUTH went dry as static crackled in his headset and the satellite image of the warehouse turned into an intense white flash on the monitor. He flung his headset on the ground, stepping back from the desk.

"How could that have happened? My entire team wiped out in a heartbeat."

Begley swung Palermo around in his seat, grabbing his shoulders and shoving him back into the desk. "And how did Foley manage to get ahead of us? Answer me!"

Palermo's mouth hung open. Before he could reply, the other computer consoles began flickering, their screens turning black.

Palermo's head swiveled to the right as an acidic odor flooded out from the mainframes. The rest of the staff began coughing, quickly shuffling towards the elevator as the room filled with smoke. A second later, the air-conditioning flowing from the overhead vents ceased while the power on the entire floor abruptly turned off, the emergency lighting panels along the floorboards illuminating.

"You said that this site was impregnable."

"It is. Whatever happened is related to a circuitry overload from our primary power source, not an internal virus."

Palermo raised his sleeve to his nose then spun around, scrutinizing the alphanumeric figures, his face looking frostbitten.

Begley's assistant tugged on his arm, coughing from the smoke. "Sir, we need to evacuate, but the elevator isn't operational."

He shook her hand free, looking at the petrified faces around the room. Begley felt his chest aching, like his ribs were constricting.

Several of his staffers rushed to the north windows, shouting about a cluster of FBI vehicles that had flooded into the parking lot, dozens of heavily armed agents moving towards the front doors.

"Everyone get to the break room in back. That should be free of smoke," said Begley. "I'll get the elevator operational then deal with the feds, so just stay calm."

Once everyone had dispersed, he grasped Palermo by the collar. "Grab everything you can related to Magellan then meet me in my office."

As Palermo went to work, rifling through his desk for backup drives and hard copies of his notes, Begley trotted with his bodyguard, Karl, to his office at the east end of the floor.

Once inside, he slid open his desk drawer, removing a pistol attached to the underside then squatting down, peeling back a pre-cut section of the carpeting to access a small floor safe. Begley yanked out a pack then stood and headed to his bookcase, motioning for his hulking bodyguard to grab the other end. The two men slid it aside.

Begley removed a headlamp from his backpack, shoving

it in place over his sweating forehead then darting a quick glance down the vertical ladder.

Palermo had just entered the room, his bulging laptop bag hanging across his hip. "Holy shit, all this time this was here. You're fucking amazing."

Begley thrust his chin at the opening, gesturing for Palermo to head down. "This leads underneath the parking garage to the sewer systems, then we'll be on foot for half a mile or so. Once we exit the sewers, head your separate ways and use the evasion packages I provided you with, then wait for me to contact you."

Palermo wrestled his bulky frame through the opening then began his descent.

Begley nodded to Karl as he headed to the entrance of his office, pulling out two incendiary grenades from his pack.

"Toss one of these over by the hallway near the break room. I've gotta hit the servers with this other one just to be safe."

Karl gave him an uneasy glance. "What's going to happen to the rest of our staff?"

"Just get it done," said Begley, shuffling forward into the main computer lab. "I can't have any of them talking. Nobody's going to miss them anyway."

Begley watched the man sprint down the hallway then stop at the end thirty feet away, removing the pin from the grenade and flinging it down the right passageway. Karl pivoted then suddenly recoiled back into the wall as the full fifteen-round capacity from Begley's Glock zippered up his torso. Seconds later, an explosion rippled out through the passageway.

Begley tossed the spent gun down, clutching the

grenade in his hand while hesitating for a moment as he stared at the Magellan mainframes.

He shook his head, bile rising up in his throat. *How did it come to this?*

Begley plucked the pin from the grenade and flung it into the entrance of the server room.

He spun around, bolting for his office and slamming the thick door, then he raced towards the escape ladder, the cold air rushing up at him as he descended amidst the shock-waves rattling the walls around him.

51

CAL WALKED UP TO NOLAN, who was leaning against the front bumper of one of the Naja gang's trucks. Both men stared at the police vehicles and military personnel still cordoning off the area around Kablana.

"Wonder what the cover story will be for this one?" said Cal.

"Turf war between Russian gangsters and the Naja clan...at least that's what the agency case officer who is briefing the authorities right now told me. Looks like the head of the Najas was killed in the conflict by some shit-hot sniper, so that'll mean there's going to be even more turf wars for a while as the other clans sort out their pecking order."

Cal glanced at the M24 rifle resting on the hood behind him. "So, you do know how to use that thing."

Nolan frowned. He removed a bottle of water from his pack, gulping it down then getting inside the truck.

"Where's the rest of your crew?" said Nolan.

"They already took off, heading south. I'll meet up with 'em later."

"Need a lift or you planning to hitchhike?"

Cal walked around the other side, feeling like his aching knees, ribs and bullet-riddled shoulder had all been subjected to a car-sized vise. "I'll take a ride...as long as you can drive better than you can shoot."

"From what I've already learned about you, we'll probably be doing both anyway. I've never seen a guy with so many fucking bulls-eyes on his back. Makes me think working in Afghanistan wasn't so bad after all."

Cal extended his hand. "Thanks for swooping in at the last minute. The outcome would have been a lot different if you and your guys hadn't shown up when you did."

Nolan responded with a hearty grip. "Foley said you were probably gonna be knee-deep in the shit by the time we arrived with every thug with a gun on your tail."

"Yeah, well, thanks all the same, Eric."

"It's Derrick, actually," he said, getting into the driver's side.

"You said Eric earlier, so you need to get that squared away. Which one is it?"

"Derrick."

Cal shrugged his shoulders, climbing into the pickup. "Who would name their kid Derrick?"

Nolan gave a crooked grin, starting the engine and heading down the gravel road. "Better than Cal. What the hell is that short for? Calvin, or better yet, Caligula?"

"Calahan, after my grandfather. What about you, *Derrick*...that's short for Theodore, I believe. Is that what's on your driver's license, or is it Teddy?"

He held on to the grab bar up top as Nolan sped down the winding road that led south to Mumbai. Cal leaned into a sharp turn along a steep dropoff. "Then again, you may not have gotten your license yet."

"Hey, you can always wait around for one of those man-powered rickshaws."

Cal leaned his head out the window, the rush of cool air wafting through his hair and beard. "Right now, I could just go for a cold beer and some pizza."

"I'm sure they ain't cold, but I think I saw a few brews rolling around in the back seat."

Cal swiveled around, groaning from his injuries. He felt around in the dark, feeling a stray can rolling around beside a dufflebag. He hoisted up both, identifying the warm can as Kingfisher beer, the main alcoholic beverage found in India.

He cracked open the lid, swigging down the tepid fluid. Setting the beer down, he unzipped the bulky dufflebag, his eyes becoming saucers upon seeing the contents.

"Where did you get this truck?"

Nolan shifted into fourth gear, heading down a long open stretch of highway. "It's a loaner."

Cal tilted the opening towards Nolan, revealing bundles of foreign currency.

"Damn, that could buy a nice beach house in Mumbai."

Cal zipped it back up, shoving it onto the floor between his boots. "I can think of a much better use, trust me."

52

CITY OF JAIPUR, 110 Miles Southwest of Delhi

THREE HOURS LATER, Nolan pulled the stolen truck into a dirt parking lot, and both men grabbed their gear and headed on foot through the city for four blocks. Cal followed the former Delta operator into the rear entrance of an old hotel then down a flight of steps beneath the kitchen towards a storage room.

At the rear, Nolan passed through a long passageway that ended at a locked door with a numeric keypad.

Stepping inside the small safehouse, Cal could see that its furnishings were sparse but practical, similar to other agency safehouses he had been in and a huge improvement over the musty old British apartment he'd been using in Delhi.

Nolan dropped his backpack on the floor, removing a ruggedized laptop, which he hastily activated. Cal headed to the kitchen, grabbing a towel and some ice from the freezer and applying it to his aching ribs while eavesdropping on the SITREP being provided by Colonel Foley regarding recent events with Begley's facility being destroyed.

Nolan snapped his fingers, waving Cal over then stepping aside as Foley leaned in, his face filling the screen.

"Cal, I'm sure you heard some of that. Just know that you have the thanks of a grateful nation—though, as usual, they'll never know the disaster that was just averted. And you have my thanks and the thanks of the President, who told me to personally inform you of an official pardon awaiting you when you return."

Shepard felt his heart racing again, a flicker of hope that he thought had been extinguished beginning to surface from an alcove in his weary soul. He glanced at Nolan then back at Foley on the screen.

"I'm not sure what to say, Colonel."

"Just come home, son."

Foley moved aside a few inches as Vogel stepped into the frame. "Cal, you can stop running. The chase...the hunt...it's over."

He looked at the features of her face, a comforting sight in an otherwise brutal day. "Thanks, Lynn. Nolan told me about what Begley put you through. I'm sorry you got tied up in all of this. I'm just grateful you're alright."

"You too." She averted her eyes momentarily. "Look, Cal, there are things that I had to do to try and locate you... things that Begley was..."

"I already heard. Don't even go there, Lynn. You've always had my back, and I'll never forget what you did to help me through the darkest days of my life."

"That means more than I can tell you." Vogel leaned in closer to the screen, smiling. "I hope you'll be on the next flight back here with Nolan."

He looked at the man beside him then back at Vogel. "So, you threw in your lot with this mook? That says a lot."

She glanced at the operations room behind her. "That's still to be determined, but it's looking promising so far."

"It'd sure be good to see you on these shores soon, Cal," said Foley as he stepped back into the frame. "We have a lot to talk about, especially now that Perseus is fully operational. And when you see Viper, tell her to call me. I have an opening that could use someone with her particular skills."

"I will let her know, and I sure appreciate your offer, sir, but let me think it over. Right now, there's one more thing I have to take care of here, but I'll be in touch."

He patted Nolan on the shoulder then slung his rifle, heading to the exit.

Nolan glanced at him, raising his hands. "Guessing I shouldn't wait for you?"

Shepard already had his iPhone in his hand, calling Viper. He waved it in the air as he opened the rear door. "If you haven't heard from me by tomorrow night, then enjoy your flight back to the States." Cal stopped in the passageway. "And Derrick, thanks...for everything. I guess you're not such a bad shot after all."

Nolan's smile turned to a smirk. He waved the man off then returned to the laptop to finish with Foley.

"That wise-ass will take some getting used to," said Nolan to the colonel.

"Ah, sounds like you two have already hit it off just fine," said Foley with a chuckle.

53

Twelve Hours Later

"Sir, Senator Edgeworth is here as you requested," said President Weller's secretary before fully opening the door of the Oval Office. The woman stepped aside as the senator entered.

Weller didn't bother standing to greet his guest. "Thank you, Evelyn. That will be all for now."

"Yes, sir." The woman nodded, closing the door on her way out, glancing over at the two Secret Service agents standing across the room near the President's desk.

Weller motioned with his hand. "Nicholas, why don't you have a seat. We have much to discuss."

Edgeworth emitted a rigid smile before sitting across from Weller's desk.

"I was surprised to get your summons, sir. How may I be of service?"

"It's *about* your service that you are here, Nick."

"Oh, I don't understand." The senator glanced nervously at the agents then back at Weller.

"It's over, Nick. Your little operation with Begley. I know all about Magellan and your offshore account in the Caymans."

Edgeworth pivoted in his seat, his face growing taut. "Come again, sir." His Southern accent was more prominent than when he first sat down.

Weller picked up a manila envelope beside him, dumping out the flash-drives, copies of foreign bank statements and enlarged photos of Edgeworth's meetings with Begley.

"What the hell is going on here? None of that is mine, and those photos could be from any of a dozen documented meetings I've had with Begley over the years."

"You really want me to play the audio of you green-lighting Begley's funding requests for Magellan so you two could begin targeting private citizens?"

Weller stood up, coming around the other side and sitting on the edge of the desk inches from the senator's face. "Or we could just jump straight to the part about you turning a blind eye to the mass murder Begley was orchestrating at the Philly convention center."

Weller leaned forward, grabbing the man's shirt at the collar and twisting the fabric against his trachea. "Domestic terrorism is alive and well within my own inner circle, it appears."

Edgeworth's eyes widened. He squirmed back, gasping as Weller released his grip. "Please, sir. It wasn't like that. Yeah, I signed off on funds to back Magellan, but that was merely a program to understand trends potentially connected with social disturbances. I didn't know Begley was actually going to follow through on that Sentinel attack. I thought that was just a simulated event with his think-tank guys to test out Magellan."

Weller leaned back, folding his arms. He glanced at the Secret Service agent on his right. "Take him away. The U.S. Marshals are already waiting outside to escort him to a holding cell until his *very public* trial for sedition."

Edgeworth's mouth hung open as his face grew ashen. "No, no. Shit, there's no need for that. I'll tell you whatever you want to know, about Begley, Magellan...anything you want."

Weller raised his hand. The agent stopped beside the senator. "You can begin with Begley's network within our clandestine agencies, including any private military contractors overseas and what you know about the dead bodies found in a tunnel beneath the Philly conference center. How much you divulge and the quality of actionable intel will determine whether you leave this office in shackles or are just seen to resign from public service due to health issues."

Edgeworth dragged his coat sleeve across the beads of sweat on his face, sitting more upright as he began geysering information.

54

THE LAST TEXT Jason Begley received on his burner phone before dumping it in a trash can outside of his hotel was from Senator Edgeworth, who asked him if he knew why the President had summoned him to the White House.

Begley never responded.

There was no need.

The text was the sole barometric indicator that the weather had just turned foul in D.C. He needed to continue with his exodus from the country before every agency could scramble together teams to locate him once Edgeworth began talking.

Despite losing his teams to Foley's operators and suffering the catastrophic failure of Magellan, he knew the President and his advisors were probably convening on how to circumvent an international public relations nightmare with the director of national intelligence and a popular senator connected with the House Appropriations Committee.

Edgeworth...that fat bastard probably spilled his guts to Weller before even sitting down.

An hour later, Begley was heading south in his step-daughter's blue Nissan Sentra before removing the GPS transponder. His only possession in life now was the go-bag on the seat beside him with enough cash, diamonds and assorted passports to start over in any of a half-dozen countries.

Pulling off the interstate near Fredericksburg, he drove for two miles then pulled into the parking lot of an abandoned strip mall. Heading to the rear, he saw Palermo's black Escalade in the distance.

The cyber expert flashed his lights twice then met Begley at the halfway point beside a dumpster.

Begley rolled his tinted window down as Palermo got out of his car and came up alongside him, squatting down by the Nissan. "Did you torch everything else you had that was connected with Magellan?"

"Yeah, boss."

Palermo removed a hard-drive from his jacket, handing it to Begley. "This contains the basic structure of the Magellan software. It will probably take about six months to get something up and running, but there's enough of the seed program there to make that happen if you decide to go down that road again." The portly man looked around the parking lot. "What now?"

"I'm on to other shores, then I'll regroup for a few months."

Begley reached out a shaky arm, giving the man a wispy handshake. "I want to thank you for your service. You are a true patriot, and I will see that you are rewarded, Dennis."

Palermo stood up, nodding. "It was my pleasure, sir. We could have really..."

The three 9mm rounds to his chest from Begley's pistol drove the man back into the Escalade. Palermo clutched the leaking holes in his sternum, blood gurgling from his trembling lips. He tried to stagger towards the shooter but collapsed back into his vehicle, sliding down the side of the Escalade onto the pavement.

"Like I said, a true patriot, dying for the cause."

Begley rolled up the window then drove away from the blighted strip mall, retracing the route back to the interstate then continuing south towards Richmond, where a private jet bound for the Caribbean was awaiting his arrival. With the hard-drive containing the schematics for the Magellan program, he at least had the framework to begin anew, selling his services on the dark web or becoming a technology broker overseas in nations with more flexible underground economies.

He heard his burner phone in the cupholder ring. He gazed down at it like the device was about to implode.

There isn't a soul on Earth who knows that number.

Begley answered it, slowly pressing it to his ear. A familiar voice stabbed through his psyche.

"Jason, we missed you at the Capitol today. Shame you couldn't attend your send-off party during your last week of work. I'm sure everyone would've been intrigued to hear more about your illegal pet project Magellan."

He gulped. "Foley, how the fuck did you get this number?"

"Perseus is even more impressive than I imagined. You should see what we're planning to do with it. But then, you can't, since you're a fugitive who betrayed his own country and President."

He narrowed his eyes, tightening his grip on the phone until it felt like it would crumble. "Ryan...I figured you were the one who initiated the virus on the Magellan servers."

"That's all you care about? That you were caught? What about the attack you arranged with Sentinel, their members you killed and all the lives that would have been lost because of you and Edgeworth?"

"You think because you have Perseus fully operational that you're some kind of hero. You're a dinosaur, Ryan, and that machine will soon replace you and the rest of the door-kickers working for you. The future of warfare is in intelligence and cyber skills, not pulling a fucking trigger and jumping from planes, old man."

"I think it's going to be all of those things actually, at least with how we hunt you down. You see, I would have been more than content to turn over your apprehension to the agency, but when you put Vogel and Shepard in the crosshairs, you entered shark-infested waters. So you can revel in your escape, if that actually comes to pass, but one night when you're half asleep in whatever third-world country you're holed up in, we'll come for you.

"And Jason...it won't be a capture mission."

The phone went silent. Begley pulled it back, staring at the device like it was leaking radiation. He rolled down the window, flinging it onto the highway then punching the accelerator, repeatedly glancing in the rearview mirror as his mouth grew dry.

FOLEY SET THE PHONE DOWN, glancing over at Vogel and West, who had heard the conversation unfold. "While we have a new mission to focus on, I still want Begley kept on your radar. There is a burn notice on him with every intelligence agency around the world, and my guess is he's heading to an extradition-free country to lay up until he can utilize some of his old contacts in the private contracting world, assuming he's able to slip away from our shores."

West scratched his forehead then sheepishly raised his hand. "Uhm, sir, there's something else we need to discuss."

He pointed to a new image he'd pulled up on his laptop, showing a district on the eastern edge of Moscow. "Hamill, who worked the Russian field office for years, got word from an old asset that a cyber firm there had a meltdown of epic proportions yesterday."

Foley stepped closer, squinting at the image on the screen. "That resembles the SAT images from the Magellan site."

West nodded. "Exactly, but this is from the Tokenoff cyber firm. And Hamill indicated it's rumored to be owned by the Orlov crime syndicate."

Foley shook his head. "Fuck...that's the place Cal said Zemenova worked for."

"And where Perseus' source code originated," said Vogel.

West tapped his pen on the screen, tracing a red line emanating from the technical college in Kablana and ending at Begley's facility. "I reviewed yesterday's events and discovered that a trace signal of the malware that nuked Magellan was also sent to the location in Moscow." He looked up at Foley. "Zemenova piggybacked off the system in India to send the same weaponized malware over to the Orlovs."

The colonel rubbed the back of his neck, a wolfish grin creeping out as he glanced up at Vogel, who had a similar expression.

"Damn, she slid that by all of us in the chaos of battle... now that is a cunning warrior," said Foley.

"Sure you don't need one more person on your team?" she said.

He flared an eyebrow. "A former Russian cyber expert with ties to the mob? I think I've asked the President for enough favors lately."

55

Mumbai

CAL WALKED down the moonlit pier to where four figures were standing near a moored sailboat.

"Everything go alright on the drive down here?" said Viper.

"Yep, just lots to think over."

"Sure you don't want to come with us? We've still got room, and the beaches in Thailand are great this time of year."

"I'm good, thanks. Think I'll head out on my own for a while. I need to clear my head and...and, well, just think about what happens next."

He glanced over at the loaded boat then to the two Syrian men, seeing Aden with a crutch under his arm to support his injured leg.

Cal removed the bulky dufflebag from his shoulder and gave it to the man, then patted the weathered figure on the arm, extending handshakes to both of the warriors. "I will forever be indebted to you, and I don't take such things lightly. If you need me at any time, regardless of the location or what's going down, you call me, and I will be on your doorstep in no time."

The men nodded, Sayyid unzipping the dufflebag and smiling as he glanced at the bundles of money that Cal had acquired from the Naja clan.

"You didn't have to do this, but it is most welcome. We would have stayed in the fight with you as long as was needed because of what you've done to help our sestra over the years."

"I appreciate that. I really do. And, yeah, Samira is like a kid sister to me too, and she usually does need a lot of help."

Cal nudged Viper with his elbow. "By the way, when you are done with your little siesta in Thailand, Foley said to call him."

"About?" she said.

"Sounds like employment. He wants his star female operative back."

"Really? That sounds enticing but also a little unnerving if he's running the shop again. You gonna join the show?"

He rubbed his chin. "Not sure, maybe do some freelance work. I just don't know."

Samira rested her hand on his cheek, smiling. "Remember that you don't always have to walk alone in the shadows. We already do enough of that in our line of work."

"Yeah, don't worry. I'll call you in a few weeks to check in...or if I need a bossy hot-head."

"And I'll text you if I ever need a reckless smart-ass."

She pulled Cal in close, giving him a long embrace.

For the first time in weeks, he felt his defenses lowering and marveled that such a feat was even possible. Cal returned the embrace, her warmth and sincerity awakening a sliver of faith that he thought had been permanently extinguished.

She pulled back, patting him on the arm, then joined the other men in the boat.

Cal glanced over at Zemenova, who was putting some water bottles in her pack. "I heard you are going to accompany Samira and her friends to Thailand for a while."

"Just to Bangkok, then I'm not sure where I'll go after that. I just know I'm done with the cyber world. The real world is where I want to spend my days for good." She looked over at the fang-like crescent moon over the bay. "And honestly, I've been on the run and living under a false identity for so long that I'm not sure what to do with myself at this point.

He nodded in deep agreement then put his hand on her shoulder. "Thank you...for everything. Stephen would be proud of what you accomplished here today."

"I'm sure he is smiling down upon us right now...upon you for being such a good friend. And it sounds like his legacy will live on in Perseus."

She leaned forward, giving him a hug.

"And thanks for getting me out of some rough spots more than a few times this week," she said.

"I hope your troubles with your former employers are over, but if you ever need anything, just reach out."

She gave him a confident nod. "I appreciate that, but I suspect they won't be a problem any longer."

A HALF-HOUR LATER, he watched the outline of their boat fade into the moonlight, the sound of the waves slapping against the dock reminding him that he was truly alone.

No more chases.

No more shootouts...hopefully.

And no more deadlines.

Is it really over?

He retraced his steps to the end of the pier, staring in either direction, still feeling shackled to the past and a festering pain that never seemed to diminish in the blur of events during the past few months.

He wanted to go home, to hug his wife Cassie, but that world was gone forever. There was only the shoreline and the empty beach before him, with nothing driving him forward for the first time that he could ever recall.

No mission to recon.

No targets to eliminate.

And no one's political agenda determining my actions.

The lack of constant adrenaline coursing through his veins coupled with a slight fading of a deep rage in him made him wonder if there was actually another world beyond clandestine ops and killing.

Maybe he would just drift from country to country or become a hermit with a waist-length beard who only ventured into town a few days a month, forgetting the world of men and their horrors.

But that's not the life I am meant to live. To live all alone in a shack in the backcountry. And it's not what Cassie would have wanted.

Plus, he knew that such isolation could become its own form of self-induced purgatory, and he'd already battled enough depression and grief to last ten lifetimes.

He walked down the pier, stepping onto the beach and heading along the empty shoreline. Cal took several deep breaths, reflecting back on the presidential pardon, knowing Foley was the magician who'd risked his own reputation in pushing for such a monumental undertaking. He felt a sense of gratitude that rekindled his loyalty to the man and reminded him that the term *brothers-in-arms* would always live on with Foley at the helm of his own unit.

He glanced up at the faint moon growing higher in the sky and, after a few miles of wandering barefoot along the coast, he paused near an abandoned fishing shack nestled in the trees before a low wall of dunes. Outside was an old firepit and a faded hammock still suspended between two palm trees.

Cal inhaled the salty fragrance of the ocean, glancing up and beholding the Milky Way, feeling like he wanted to partake of this view for the rest of his days.

But he knew he'd be turning his back on the people he loved dearly and forsaking an oath to protect others that he had sworn to uphold.

First, I must sleep for a while...or a month.

He headed inland towards the shack, his steps becoming lighter and his eyes lingering upon the swaying hammock.

A WEEK LATER, in a rented beachside cabana further down the coast from Mumbai, Cal was sitting at a makeshift bamboo table and slicing open a papaya while brushing away a pesky wild parakeet that kept trying to snipe his plate full of food. He felt his cellphone vibrate in his pocket, and he knew it could only be one person.

The succinct text made Shepard's heart rate spike. A slow grin crept out from his lips while he re-read Foley's message.

Cal, could use you for some freelance work if you're up for it? Begley has just emerged on our radar and is overdue for a visit.

What do you say?

He leaned back, slipping a sweet wedge of fruit in his mouth then sliding the plate towards the eager parakeet.

"Enjoy, my little friend. I have other shores to head to, it seems."

Shepard dragged his sticky fingers across his shorts then typed his response.

Colonel, be on your doorstep shortly. I look forward to meeting your team.

And thanks for always being in my corner, sir.

Cal

56

Two Weeks Later

Barbados

Jason Begley ambled along the stern deck of his yacht, holding two cold Heineken bottles and extending one to his new bodyguard, Drake, a six-foot-four German who was seated on a wicker chair on the other side of the small round table. Both men swigged down their brews while gazing out at the ocean.

"I've got some work lined up for a few weeks at the end of this month," Begley said in an irritated tone. "My contacts in Surinam said they would have something for us shortly. Just be patient...we need to keep a low profile for a few months more. With things heating up again between the U.S. and China, the President and all of the intel agencies will be less focused on international manhunts, and we can pick up and head to Eastern Europe, where freelancing opportunities abound."

Drake finished his beer, tossing the spent bottle over the side of the vessel then getting up and stretching. "I'm gonna go over the nautical charts again."

His boss nodded his beer bottle towards the man, extending his legs out then tilting his brimmed hat down lower as he reclined in his seat. Begley heard a series of muted popping sounds followed by the warm sensation of fluid splashing on his legs.

He bolted upright, seeing Drake collapse back onto the deck, the top of his skull little more than bone splinters amidst a cascade of blood and brain matter.

Begley felt paralyzed, the beer bottle falling from his hand and shattering on the deck as he recoiled into his seat, staring at Shepard moving closer. The man kept his suppressed Glock pointed at Begley's chest.

"God, no!" Begley waved his trembling hands, his face becoming ashen. "No, no, Shepard...you don't have to do this."

Cal frowned, his wet suit still dripping with saltwater. "Of course I do. All the trails these many months have led to this moment. When Foley and Vogel told me they had located you, I knew I had to get to you before the other agencies tracked you down, putting you in a nice, comfy cell for the rest of your days. Somehow, that just doesn't suit you."

Shepard drove a vicious backhand across the man's face, sending him crashing to the deck. "That one's for Vogel and the hell you put her through."

Begley slithered along the floor, his head throbbing. Instinctively, he reached for the sheath knife on his belt, but he was met by the crushing force of Shepard's boot smashing down onto his hand.

"Fuck!" He rolled to the side, clutching his broken wrist.

Shepard removed the blade, flinging it over the side of the yacht. "Get up or I'll break your other hand, then work my way down the line until you resemble a jellyfish."

Begley struggled to stand, leaning against the railing as Shepard prodded him forward along the walkway. "We need to have a little talk about how much classified intel you've divulged since leaving your old job."

———

THE SUN WAS ALMOST at the horizon when Cal emerged from the surf, carrying his fins and unslinging the O2 tank on his back. He trudged through the sandy shoreline, stepping up onto the band of well-worn volcanic rocks then heading up the grassy slope towards a cluster of young palm trees.

Nolan extended a hand out, grabbing the oxygen tank then setting it down on the ground beside his radio and binoculars.

Shepard removed his short-sleeved wetsuit, stripping down to his swim trunks then grabbing a tan shirt out of the open backpack next to Nolan.

"You're forgetting the other post-mission critical items that I stowed in the pack," said the former Delta Force operator.

Cal thrust his hand further down into the pack, feeling something cold, and removed two cans of partially chilled Coors.

"It would seem so." He handed one to Nolan then sat down in the shade beside him and cracked open the can, sipping the welcome beverage.

The two men had their vision fixed below, watching a flock of seagulls dive-bombing the army of crabs between the rocks and the retreating shoreline.

"How'd the ribs and arm recover after India?" said Nolan.

"Better than I thought, but it helped not to be jumping out of planes or carrying a fifty-pound ruck and rifle for a while."

"You know, I can teach you a few self-defense moves so you don't get banged up again. You really should know how to handle yourself better in a fight."

Shepard almost choked on his beer. He wiped his lips, letting out a chuckle. "I'm honored that you would take time out from your busy schedule polishing weapons in the armory to share your Call of Duty moves."

Cal unzipped a side pouch on the pack, removing a cell-phone and pressing the singular number on it.

"I've obtained a few flash-drives from Begley's safe, one of which had a breakdown of a recent transaction for a large, illegal weapons shipment going down in Africa that you might want to look into."

"Indeed," Vogel said.

Cal gazed out over the ocean, his eyes settling on the vessel. "The package is gift-wrapped," he said. "I thought you would want the honors."

"You can count on it," said Vogel in a stern voice. He heard her punch in the five-digit code, initiating the cell-phone detonator on the other end of the brick of C4 secured to Begley's bound figure on the yacht four miles distant from the shoreline.

He glanced at Nolan then out at the ocean as an explosion sliced out across the serene vista. Both men remained transfixed on the forty-foot vessel erupting in flames as wood and steel shrapnel flew skyward. A few minutes later, the smoldering remains of the yacht sank below the surface, and the ocean returned to its former pristine self.

Shepard finished his beer then stood up, grabbing his gear while Nolan slung the backpack over his bare shoulder.

"How do you think Jason Begley's departure from this world will be recorded in the annals of the intelligence community?" said Nolan. "Will people in the know say it was a well-deserved fate catching up with him here, or will he just receive a notable mention as an esteemed public servant who retired to more distant shores?"

Shepard glanced back at the former location of the boat then continued walking along the white sugar-sand.

"Jason who?"

Nolan grinned.

Arriving back at their jeep along the dirt road, the two men stowed their items in the back then climbed inside. Nolan started the engine, blasting the air-conditioning, and turned the vehicle around to do the nine-mile drive back to the airfield east of Bridgetown on the other side of Barbados.

Nolan's iPhone rang, and he put it on speaker.

"How's the sightseeing going there, lads?" said Foley. "I heard you got in some time on the water."

"Yeah, the trip was very rewarding," said Cal. "The sea is much calmer now than it was a few hours ago."

"Then that concludes your travel plans, gentlemen. And remember, Cal, you've got an open invitation at any time. We, *I*...would certainly welcome you fulltime rather than just freelancing it."

Cal looked out the window, watching a group of pelicans in the distance bobbing along the waves.

"I appreciate the offer, Colonel. The weather down here

is pretty good this time of year, and I think I'll do some island-hopping for a while. Maybe see the Caribbean for a bit...but I'll be in touch if I change my mind."

"You know how to find me, Cal. Take care, son, and remember, you've always got a helping hand any time it's needed."

"Copy that, sir."

"Nolan...keep me apprised of your findings on the next leg of your journey," said Foley. "We can be wheels-up in a matter of hours and relocate to your position, depending on what you discover."

"I will check in with you in two days, Colonel."

The call ended. Shepard picked up a water bottle from the floor and guzzled down the fluid. "Heading off on another government-sponsored vacation for a while?"

"Yep. I'd read you in on it, but it sounded like you're not on the team...yet."

"The ticket in your pack indicated that Panama is your next stop after this, so nice job with the OP-SEC there, buddy."

"Just one stop of many in Latin America."

"If you're hanging around those parts, that can only mean narco-traffickers or weapons dealers."

"You're overlooking the lucrative trade in endangered reptiles. I'm going deep cover into the illicit world of boa-constrictor smuggling."

"Good luck with that. Your choice of aftershave should prevent you from suffering any bites."

Nolan came to a four-way stop, the roads empty in every direction. He put the vehicle in park, pivoting towards Shepard.

"I could totally see you living like a surfer down here, letting your hair grow out so you can thread in some beads to help you blend in with the other expats in your turtle-rescue group."

Shepard shook his head. "At least I can grow a beard. Maybe you'll see what that's like once you hit adolescence." He thrust his chin at the open road ahead. "Flight. Airfield. Remember?"

Nolan reluctantly engaged the clutch and put it in first gear, proceeding forward. "Come on, man...what Foley is offering is an operator's dream come true. And you already know the guy, so he'll cut you a lot of slack."

Cal looked over at the endless miles of sand dunes, knowing Nolan was right. "Sounds like *you* are the one who could use someone watching over your top-knot, or what little there is with that receding hairline."

"It'd be a week of work, and I'll keep your name off the books with Foley, if you'd like. If the team ends up in my AO, then you'd be free to surf off into the sunset and go your own way."

He rubbed the stubble on his chin. "Not much of a surfer. That's Viper's thing. But you could probably use someone to provide overwatch for a few days at this *non-Panama* location. After that, I'll see where things are headed, but a week is all for now."

"A month it is then." Nolan grinned, manipulating the stick then speeding down the dirt road. "And I hope you like pork-chatas, 'cause I live on the stuff when I'm down in Latin America."

"The hell is that?"

"Pork chops marinated in rum and horchata, baby...my own recipe. Though with your delicate constitution, I may have to leave out the liquor until you can build up a tolerance."

Shepard laughed, seeing the operator suddenly loosen up. "So how long does it take to build up a tolerance to *you*?"

Nolan smacked him on the shoulder. "Hell, buddy, I tend to rub off easily on people, making them *better* than they were before."

Cal chuckled again, leaning back. "Yeah, that's what really worries me...and your definition of 'better.'"

He wanted to say more, keep up the banter and laughter. Instead, he looked out at the sea of silent dunes, enjoying the camaraderie with someone who had come to his aid with a lifesaving shot during a dire situation that could have had a different outcome.

People like Foley, Vogel, Viper, and now Nolan were part of a small inner circle of warriors that he could let his guard down with long enough to joke and slap each other's backs, knowing that he could rely on them like few others when the storm clouds gathered on life's horizon. He had been given a second chance for a new life, and while he wasn't sure what that would look like, he knew the people he wanted to spend it with.

He eased back in the seat, his shoulders relaxing. Cal thrust his chin at the open road ahead.

"Latin America it is then, amigo...and may God help me survive your cooking."

THE END

Continue on with Cal Shepard in Volume 3, *Critical Response*. Join my email list on my website below and you can grab a FREE short story, *Lethal Conduct*, which recounts Cal Shepard's harrowing mission in Africa with his former Search & Destroy Unit.

You can also keep updated with current happenings at JTSawyer.com or on Facebook at JTSawyerBooks.

Lastly, as an Indie writer, your feedback is critical to refining my craft. If you wouldn't mind posting a review on Amazon, I'd be grateful! Reviews make a world of difference in the life of a writer and help direct other readers to our works.

ADDITIONAL TITLES BY JT SAWYER

Dead In Their Tracks: The Mitch Kearns Combat Tracker Series, Volumes 1-12

Meet Mitch Kearns, a former Special Forces Combat Tracker who works for the FBI hunting down notorious criminals. Crossing paths with Israeli agent Dev Leitner, the two seasoned operators join forces to bring down terrorist cells, rogue assassins, and black-ops mercenaries in these adrenaline-soaked novels that span the globe.

THE EMERGENCE SERIES, VOLUMES 1-8

An epic struggle for survival between humans and a twisted mutation of undead begins in *Emergence* when a deadly virus, originating in China, quickly spreads throughout the world, turning humans into cunning predators with interconnected mental abilities. The human race is about to become an endangered species unless CIA Agent Will Reisner and his elite team can track down the source of the virus before the world is completely consumed. If you liked *The Puppet Masters, I am Legend,* or *The Strain* then check out Emergence!

ABOUT THE AUTHOR

JT Sawyer is the pen name for Tony Nester. Before becoming a fulltime writer, JT made his living teaching survival courses for the military special operations community, Department of Homeland Security, US Marshals, FAA, and other federal agencies throughout the country. He has appeared on the Travel Channel, Fox News, Discovery, in the New York Times and served as a consultant for the film *Into the Wild* along with being the author of 12 non-fiction books on bushcraft and survival. Nowadays, JT prefers having a roof over his head and placing his fictional characters in dire situations in his thriller and post-apocalyptic books. He lives with his family in Colorado Springs, CO. Visit jtsawyer.com for more information.

Made in the USA
Middletown, DE
06 July 2022

68661734R00165